Danger
In The Hills

JODI BURNETT

JODI BURNETT

Cover Art by Oliviaprodesign

Jodi-Burnett.com

BOOKS by JODI BURNETT

Letting Go

<u>Flint River Series</u>

Run For The Hills
Hidden In The Hill
Danger In The Hills

JODI BURNETT

DEDICATION

To all the federal, state, and local law enforcement
officers who keep us safe day in and day out.
Thank you.

JODI BURNETT

ACKNOWLEDGMENTS

First, I thank the good Lord for blessing me with work I love, and for the inspiration with which to do it.

I am enormously appreciative for my team. A huge thanks to Chris, Emily M., Sarah, Jenni R., Jenn V., Kae, and Barb, who helped me shape my rough manu-script.

Thanks to Sheri, Emily B., and Jymn, my dedicated critique partners who watched over my every word. You continue to inspire and teach me much about writing, dedication, and perseverance. I'm grateful for your wisdom, support, and friendship.

Another big thanks to my editor, Cate Byer, for her expertise and guidance. Cate, your sharp eye and attention to detail are priceless.

I could not do without the support and encouragement of my family. Thank you all for pushing me and laughing with me. I love each of you beyond measure.

Of course, my greatest appreciation is for my husband Chris, whose strength keeps me going and whose business sense is invaluable! Thanks for all you do, honey! I love you.

JODI BURNETT

CHAPTER 1

Deep in the woods of northern Idaho, Special Agent Jack Stone peered through his Steiner M830r binoculars at the neo-Nazi compound situated two hundred and fifty feet below. Winter glided in on a sleigh of frigid, pine-scented wind. Ice and snow already capped the high peaks. The rocky, cold ground pressed its sharp edges into his skin as he surveilled his quarry. His legs ached, and he flexed his feet to relieve the pin-pricking sensation caused by lack of circulation. Jack adjusted his position and squinted against the early morning sun for a better focus on the rogue militia's hidden camp. He observed the encampment at the base of the mountain in silence as the residents began to stir and start their daily routines.

Three days ago, the FBI hostage negotiators contacted the guards at the front gates of the barricaded compound. Their request that the women and children who lived there be sent out went unheeded. Two days ago, in conjunction with ATF and Homeland Security, the FBI shut down all electrical power to the camp. However, because the group of radicals was prepared to live completely off the grid, they simply flipped on their generators and went about their business as usual. Today, two FBI SWAT teams were poised to force the compound leaders into compliance.

The Special Agent in Command briefed all the men at the basecamp located ten miles down the canyon before the two teams took up their mountainside positions. "Everyone remain calm and stay alert. Our goal is to slow things down—to negotiate. Ideally, without any weapons fired. Let's get them talking about their motivations." The SAC tapped his fingers on a map covering the table. His command voice drilled on. "Remember, we're here because this group has taken terrorist action against American citizens. We are *not* here because their ideology differs from ours. There are women and innocent children inside. Do not fire unless your life is in imminent danger. That being said, be safe and consider *everyone* inside a possible threat."

At least they'd been briefed ahead of time about the families. Jack's gut bunched when he thought of breaching a site with kids inside. He scratched at his dark morning stubble. It sickened him, what some adults did to their children. Maybe they'd free them in time for their brainwashing to be reversed.

Agent Stone raised his binoculars again when he noticed a young woman cross the courtyard. Their informant hadn't mentioned any younger women. The females in the encampment were all supposedly 35 years or older, and all of them mothers of young or teenaged kids. This woman looked to be in her early to mid-twenties and moved with an easy grace. His gaze followed her across the grounds to a lean-to shack. She disappeared inside.

Jack's partner, Rick Sanchez, sat leaned back against a rock outcropping twenty-feet behind him and to his left. Jack glanced back at his friend. "Hey, did you see that woman?"

"Yeah, baby. Didn't know these backwoods Nazi girls were so good-looking." Rick smirked.

Jack shook his head and grinned. "Right? I don't remember any briefing on a young woman her age, though."

"For sure. We should have been given a deck of identification cards, like in Afghanistan."

"Shut up, I'm serious. Who do you suppose she is?"

"Hell, I don't know. Guess we'll find out."

Jack nodded and scanned the compound one more time. There was no one he trusted more to watch his six than Rick Sanchez, and he was glad to have him there. They'd become close friends after they met at the FBI Academy. The two competed fiercely to be top-dog in both academics and physical challenges. Their inner-branch rivalry gave them even more common ground as they argued about who was better, Rick's Marine Corps or Jack's Army. They started out as rivals and ended up as friends who trusted and respected each other immensely.

The raid commander had ordered the FBI teams to sit tight and observe only, until further notice. Jack waited for the breach order to come down the pike. He expected to hear something around midnight. His team practiced raids like this continually, so with precision timing, surprise, and some luck, they'd be able to capture the men and isolate their families—hopefully without injury. Their foremost objective was to capture Jedediah Hotchkiss, the compound leader, and Roger MacNeil, his second-in-command. Then they would search the compound for irrefutable evidence that linked this terrorist group to the thwarted bombing of an elementary school in Chicago two months ago. Jack shuddered knowing a mere fluke of intelligence had tipped them off and prevented the explosion and subsequent death of hundreds of innocents.

Static from wind blowing across someone's mic sounded in his earpiece before the voice of Team Two's leader spoke. "The numbers Werner gave us seem to be fairly accurate. We do not have a confirmed number of children, but family and militant numbers are close to what we expected."

"Roger that," Jack agreed. "As soon as I receive orders, we'll move in on my signal." Several voices acknowledged his command. Jack held up his binoculars and continued to observe. "Remember, there are families down there. The last thing we want is another Waco or Ruby Ridge. As of now, we are EMCON until oh-one-hundred hours."

The encampment occupants went about their daily business. The early winter chill mostly kept everyone indoors, except for a group of kids that ran about playing hide-and-seek after lunchtime. Otherwise, the camp sat quiet. Smoke drifted up from chimneys. It seemed as if no one knew they were surrounded by FBI SWAT teams.

Dusk descended, and with it came lower temperatures and hunger. No matter the circumstances, blazing heat or bitter cold, the body always demanded fuel. Field stakeouts didn't come with music, fast food, and a cup of coffee though, and he hankered for the caffeine. What little activity they witnessed in the camp settled down with the evening, and the inviting scent of dinners baking in ovens drifted up the hill.

Rick tossed a rock at Jack to get his attention. "That food smells so damn good. Are you sure we have to wait to raid?"

Jack chuckled. "You think that smells good? You should smell my gran's lasagna. Man, when we were kids, nothing brought us in from playing as fast as the smell of Italian sausage, tomatoes, and melted cheese. And her garlic bread—oh God." His stomach rolled in on itself and grumbled. He reached into his tactical pack and pulled out an MRE—a Meal-Ready-to-Eat—and a bottle of water. Tonight's selection—reconstituted beef stew.

The aroma wafting up the mountain turned his thoughts to home and to his brothers, Cade and Trent. He had recently reunited with them and his grandma, Mary, after not seeing any of them in almost ten years. He and Trent had fought over the future of the family ranch, and Jack left for West Point without ever making things right between them. They still had some unresolved issues, but he would deal with all of that when this case ended.

Jack had been hoping to make it back home to Flint River in time to stand up with Trent at his wedding. It wasn't likely, though, this situation was dragging out much longer than they expected, and Trent planned to marry his childhood sweetheart in two days. He couldn't contact his family in the middle of a mission and he sure as hell didn't want Trent to take him not showing up to the wedding as another insult. There was already too much pain and misunderstanding to wade through.

Jack glanced at his watch. They had another six hours to sit and wait. He flexed each muscle group in turn, working to stay at the ready. By nightfall, the only movement down below came from two perimeter patrol guards and the lookouts posted on top of four guard towers built at each corner of the fortress.

Jack's radio crackled and the SAC's rough voice came across the line. "Agent Stone, give the order for the raid at oh-one-hundred-hours. Do you copy?"

"Copy that, sir. Out."

At precisely 1:00 a.m., Jack broke radio silence, and in a harsh whisper, ordered his team to advance on the stronghold. He stretched his stiffened muscles and moved in silence down the mountainside toward the compound fence.

The militia had built the barrier wall surrounding the complex out of logs—lashed together and sharpened at their tips, similar to an old western cavalry post. They planned to maneuver close enough to verbally order the guards to drop their weapons. If they did not comply, agents would take them out. Jack's heart pounded with exhilaration. He'd waited over two months for this confrontation and it was finally here, within his grasp. These sick bastards needed to be in prison where they weren't a threat to good people—to children. He ran, crouched low, his vest heavy with grenades and ammunition. The weight of his Colt M4 carbine drawing him forward. All his senses sparked on high alert.

His men approached the perimeter unseen. With

hand signals, they communicated the movements of their choreographed attack. Agents called out to the two perimeter guards, but instead of surrendering their weapons, the guards fired at the operatives. *Damn it!* Jack hoped taking this compound would happen without casualties, but that was not going to be the case. The tower guards positioned on the corner platforms joined the action and were consequently sighted in. Six spits tore through the air and six guards fell. Agents launched smoke grenades into the compound to provide cover and prepared to breach the main gate.

The explosives team wired the barricaded entrance, then moved back to take up their offensive positions. To screen their attack, Jack's men popped more smoke grenades over the entrance and simultaneously blew the front security gate off its hinges with C-4 explosives.

"Breach. Breach now!" Jack shouted across the radio to his unit, his blood racing hot. Agents rushed into the fortification, alternating right and left, covering each other as they took up their new positions. A man stationed at the community building door fired at the officers and they blew him off the porch. Following the initial shots, the night exploded into live fire. Shots flew out of every structure on the grounds.

"Flank the main building and secure it. Then light it up."

"What about the kids, sir?" An anonymous voice whispered into his earpiece.

"Use concussion grenades." Jack didn't know where the kids were and it made him uneasy. He presumed they were in their own houses and hoped their parents had them safely tucked away. "As soon as the grenades go off, enter and take the bunker. Secure and search everyone, even kids. I don't want to lose any of our guys tonight. Take nothing for granted."

Jack took cover behind a wooden fence that marked a garden and peered around it, rifle ready. Shots erupted into the night. Air, sharpened by bullets that barely missed him, stung his face. Jack squatted low to the ground and signaled to his partner crouched across from him, asking for cover. Rick nodded once, his dark eyes brimming with adrenaline. Jack sprinted to a position behind a large shipping container that served as a house standing thirty-yards away. Bullets zipped through the air, but his cover held and Jack made it to the new spot unharmed. Jack then laid down a cover of bullets in return for Rick, giving back what he had received seconds ago. The metallic tang of gunpowder burned the back of his throat.

Both men crept around behind the house, making their way toward the large structure. The common area in the center of the compound contained the heat of the battle. The neo-Nazi militants waged their greatest defense from the centralized building, presumably where the leaders, Hotchkiss and MacNeil, were holed up.

As they neared the alleyway that led them to the headquarters, Jack heard growling. The savage snarling and barking of a pack of fierce dogs locked in kennels escalated into a frenzy. Jack was surprised the animals were contained. These people clearly weren't expecting a raid, and he was thankful the dogs were caged in so they wouldn't have to shoot them.

Moonlight flashed off the dogs' glistening fangs and powerful jaws. Jack resisted flinching at the angry and frustrated canines charging their chain-link barrier. He motioned for Rick to cover him and he ran toward the side of the big lodge.

The partners proceeded in their alternating pattern until they were both close enough to the firestorm to launch smoke and concussion grenades inside the main hall. Agents with filtered respirators poured inside after the detonations that temporarily halted the resistance, allowing the operatives to apprehend the shooters.

Militiamen fired from their steel-sided homes, pinning Jack, Rick, and a small group of men to the side of the building. Other agents used the distraction to swing around and approach their targets from behind. They launched concussion grenades into the housing containers and teams followed, taking control of each residence. The FBI subdued militia members, binding their wrists together with zip-ties. After a quick sweep, they confiscated all weapons and marched the captives out to the common area in the village center.

"Where are the children?" Jack shouted to a group of agents who shook their heads and shrugged, unknowing.

"Maybe we got bad intel," an agent suggested.

Jack shook his head. He knew there were kids in the camp. He'd seen them playing. Jack approached one of the bound women standing under guard. "Where are they?"

She stared at him defiantly, but said nothing.

Jack turned to two other operatives. "Find the kids," he yelled.

"There's no one left in the bunker." An agent clad in all black called out.

Jack bounded up the steps to the central building and paced the porch. He stopped and called out. "Check to see if the houses have underground bunkers."

Men dispersed to the steel storage containers converted into homes in search of any secret openings or hidden spaces below. Before long a voice called out, "Found some!" The agent ushered three kids of varying ages outside. "They were hiding down below. We think a series of tunnels connect the bunkers together." The agent handed off the children and turned back inside to help his team.

The smallest child in the trio, maybe five, cried out and ran across the open area to her mother. Her siblings followed, looking sheepish. As teams discovered more kids hidden below, they filtered out from the converted storage containers.

After agents frisked everyone, including the children, and confiscated anything that could be used as a weapon, the kids were allowed to go to their mothers. They escorted families out into the compound yard where bright lights illuminated the clearing. They dragged and shoved the shooters into the open space as well, then took an official count. Ten women and seventeen minors were taken into custody. There were twenty-two militiamen alive and six casualties, but the two leaders the FBI informant told them about were unaccounted for. Jack also noted there was no sign of the young dark-haired woman he observed early yesterday morning. That meant at least three people were missing.

"Where are Jedediah Hotchkiss and Roger

MacNeil?" He paced in front of the subdued militiamen who'd been forced to kneel on the ground with their hands on their heads.

Eyes flashed at him or stared down at the dirt, but no one answered.

Jack's neck and shoulders bunched with frustration. He shouted to a contingent of his men, "Run another search through every structure and hiding space. Find them." A small unit separated from the group to locate the missing pair of neo-Nazi terrorist leaders.

An agent approached him. "Sir, we found a building that's been recently used as a stable. No horses or mules in there now, but it looks like there has been within the last couple of days."

"Do you keep horses at this facility?" Jack asked the captives. They continued to watch him without speaking.

Half an hour later, the search team reported back. "We didn't find anyone else, sir. The two leaders are gone. But, we did find a tunnel that leads out from the main building. It goes under the gate and lets out about a half-mile up into the hills."

"Shit! Find them! Apprehending those men is the primary focus of this entire mission." Jack ground his teeth and chewed his lower lip. "I saw a young woman with long dark hair inside the camp yesterday. She's also missing."

A female agent approached Jack with a girl who looked about twelve. "Sir, this is Joy. She told me she helped a woman named Laurel care for a horse, but she doesn't know where either of them are now."

Jack squatted down. "What color is the horse?"

The girl offered a shy smile, her teeth a stark

white in her dirt-smudged face. "Wisaka? She's a paint."

He smiled at Joy. "You didn't see Laurel go anywhere with Wisaka?"

Joy's eyes were big and round in her young face. She shook her head.

"When did you last see Wisaka?"

"Couple a·days ago."

Jack nodded and patted the girl's shoulder wanting her to feel safe. "Thanks, Joy. Will you let us know if you remember anything else about them?" *How the hell did they sneak a horse out of the compound?*

He stood and turned back to his men. "We are looking for two men in their fifties or sixties who may be with a young dark-haired woman in her twenties. It's possible they have a horse. The sooner we start tracking them the better. There's no time to waste."

CHAPTER 2

J ack ordered several agents on his team to take mothers, one at a time, to gather coats, clothing, baby items, and any other necessities they needed for their imminent removal from the compound. A freshman agent, and recent addition to Jack's team, approached him. He adjusted his helmet. "What'll happen with all these people, sir?"

"We'll keep the men and women separate and they'll all be retained and processed." Jack glanced toward the gates. "The crisis response teams should be here soon. They'll take the women and children by bus to the FBI satellite location in Coeur d'Alene."

The young agent's brow furrowed, and he continued to stare Jack in the eye.

"What's wrong?"

"How do we know all the women are innocent? I mean they all live here together, they must agree with the dogma."

"We're not assuming they're innocent, don't worry. In fact, every compound resident, both male and female, will receive medical and psych evals. Adults will be interviewed to determine the depth of their individual involvement in the terrorist plots. After that they'll either be arrested and jailed, or meet with reintegration experts in the hope of keeping families together."

"What happens to the kids if their parents are arrested?"

Jack leveled his gaze at the young agent. "They'll be handed over to family services, and probably put into foster care."

The young man nodded and glanced away.

"It's not ideal, but I'm proud none of the moms or kids were hurt during the raid." Jack clasped the man's shoulder. "We're not the ones who put these kids in this situation. We're doing the best we can for them at this point."

"Yes, sir."

Fresh agents were dispatched to search the premises and manage the detainees. Mission coordinators assembled tables covered with food and hot drinks and set up two rows of cots in the main building so the assault teams could warm up and rest. Jack, trained by his years in the army could sleep anywhere, anytime. He managed about three hours of shut-eye before he was ready to get back to work.

As the sun peeked over the eastern horizon, peach and cobalt tendrils of light stretched across the morning sky. Agents gained zero information from their initial contact with militia members about where their leaders had bugged-out to. These followers were loyal to a fault. As others investigated the compound for evidence connecting this group with the bombing in Chicago, Jack and Rick, both highly-trained trackers, prepared to hunt down Hotchkiss, MacNeil, and the missing woman.

The frosty morning air bit Jack's cheeks. Though it was only the end of November, winter made her intentions known in the high-country. The forecast promised the day would be sunny and a bit warmer until sundown, so Jack chose his lighter-weight jacket. With any luck, he and the rest of the search team would make quick work of finding the missing fugitives and they'd be enjoying an icy beer next to a bright, hot fire by happy hour.

Assuming the leaders escaped during the attack the previous night, the team divided into fourths. Each pair of agents searching in a different direction. Jack and Rick were assigned the northern side. They planned to start their hunt at the mouth of the underground tunnel. But first, they searched around the rear gate for evidence of the woman and her horse. Finding their route proved impossible. There were tons of broken branches, displaced stones, and scuffs in the soil. It looked to be an area where children played during the day and hoof prints and horse manure were scattered in all three directions.

Noting the trails leading into the thick woods, Jack said, "Let's take each path up about a mile. Hopefully, we'll find something telling a little farther away from the camp."

Rick nodded. He swiped a shock of black hair out of his eyes and took off up the path on the far right. Jack headed up the middle one. He kept his pace slow and painstaking. Finding no fresh tracks, he sighed and signaled Rick on the radio to meet him at the starting point. Rick met him back at the trailhead and together they took the third path on the left.

"I'm not finding anything. You?"

Rick shook his head. "I radioed the team to see if anyone's seen anything. Sounds like there's lots of prints but it's hard to say how old they are. They're following every possible lead."

At the half-mile point, Jack and Rick found the escape tunnel opening, but they hiked another mile before Jack stopped. He pointed to an overturned stone and subsequent scuff in the dirt. From there, they spiraled out. Their prey had left the path and moved up the hill.

"They might think they're being smart, but going off the trail makes following them easier." Jack knelt by a scrape in a carpet of pine needles. "The terrain is rugged and dense on this side of the compound. I can see how they could sneak a horse out without being seen."

"Roger that." Rick struck off to follow some marks. "Looks to me like only one set of boot-prints head this way."

"Okay, let's split for a little way. I'll continue to head up and see if I can find any other signs."

Little sleep and the drain of adrenaline caused Jack's body to feel twenty pounds heavier. After about five miles of searching, he sat on a rock under the boughs of a great pine to rest and re-fuel. He pulled out an energy bar and tore open the wrapper. Jack eyed his watch and shook his head. It was already thirteen-hundred hours and they hadn't found anything substantial. He rubbed the back of his neck and stood to stretch when his radio squawked.

"Stone, you copy?"

"Stone here."

"I've got him. I've got MacNeil."

"What's your twenty? Do you need backup?"

"Negative. This scruffy little runt won't give me any trouble."

"Roger that. Does he say he was with Hotchkiss?"

"He's not talking, other than confirming his name."

"Figures. Good work, Sanchez. Sure you don't want help?"

"Nope. I've got this puke."

Jack chuckled. "You take MacNeil down to headquarters. I'll cut across in your direction and try to pick up mini-Hitler's tracks further up the ridge."

"The official trail ends where I found him."

"Okay, I'll track the back country, due north from there."

"Roger that, Jack. I'll catch up to you once I drop MacNeil off at headquarters. Leave me some crumbs to follow."

"Will do, Gretel." Jack chuckled. "Out."

Jack repacked his bag and continued up the hill. As he hiked, the forest grew thicker. Unlike his quarry, Jack left obvious signs of his own route for Rick to find. Every twenty feet, he pushed a bamboo marker fitted with fluorescent orange ribbon into the dirt. Rick could easily follow him and they would collect the markers on the way back down.

He pushed pine boughs out of his face and ducked below the branches of deciduous trees. A flicker of silver caught his eye, and he stopped. He softened his gaze trying to locate what he had seen. He reached out to lift several strands of long, colorless hair fluttering in the breeze from a branch on his left. Pinpricks of excitement skittered across his skull and down his neck. Finally they had something concrete. Jack drew a small Ziploc evidence bag from the side pocket of his pack and slipped the hair inside.

Human? Or horse maybe? The hair was coarse, but not so much so he could be a hundred-percent certain it came from an animal. Besides, he hadn't seen any signs of a horse all day. No hoofprints or manure. Whoever had the horse didn't come this way. In fact, the boot prints Jack had seen were large, most likely not a woman's. By this he presumed she had the horse, and had taken a different path.

Jack studied the ground around him. *Something* left that hair on the tree. He searched to see if that something left any prints. The one photo he had seen of Jedediah Hotchkiss depicted an older man with longish, graying hair and an even longer scraggly beard. The strand certainly could have come from him. No matter, at this point, it was all he had to go on.

A broken twig drew him further. There were still no tracks on the ground, but he knew he was on someone's trail. If his luck held out, it would lead him to Hotchkiss. A Steller's Jay cried out as Jack stepped off in the direction of his prey and he paused for a few seconds to appreciate the beautiful dusky blue and black feathered bird.

"What have you seen up here, my friend? Too bad you can't show me where this scumbag is."

The jay cawed at him and flew up into the trees.

Jack wished he had a K-9 team with him as he scanned the mulch-covered forest floor. Not expecting to be tracking people through the woods, the FBI hadn't deployed any canines with the mission. Dogs would find their target in no time. He was confident the SAC had sent to Denver for a K-9 unit by now.

Mashed moss on a small rock outcropping convinced Jack he was on the right trail. He considered the length and direction of the scuff and determined the footfall headed north. Step by steady step, Jack followed where the signs pointed.

He pressed the talk button on the transmitter. "Sanchez, I've found his tracks." He gave the GPS coordinates on his watch and said, "I'm headed northeast from here. Stone out." He wished Rick would hurry. The sun hunkered deep in the sky on his left and the temperature dropped fast.

No reply came across the radio. Rick was most likely out of range, but his partner knew the general area where he was tracking. Jack realized he should wait for Rick before he got too far away, but finding signs was like crack and he was addicted. He couldn't resist looking for the next one. Besides, Rick would catch up soon, making much faster time since he could follow the flags and not take time looking for tracks.

He moved on, looking for the next mark. He found a line of fairly regular footprints in the mulch and Jack followed the clues easily for another several miles, or so, before the tracks disappeared into a mountain stream. His body sagged. Jack had no doubt Hotchkiss was an experienced survivalist and had hiked through the water with the single purpose of hiding his trail.

At the edge of the chortling stream, Jack squatted and studied the stones on its bed, underneath the clear, cold currents of tripping water. As he caught his breath, he noticed several stones had been dislodged up stream. He would track upstream then, monitoring both banks for signs of someone getting out of the water. A frigid wind rolled down the side of the mountain whispering that Jack should head back to camp, but he ignored the warning, not wanting to lose the trail. Besides, Rick would be there soon and had promised to bring his cold-weather gear up when he came.

Jack blew into his cupped hands to warm them before he headed up the bank. Watching for tiny signs of passage on both sides of the water was a challenge, so Jack kept his pace slow and methodical. He almost gave up and returned to the last known marker when he saw a minor tread, so small he nearly stepped on it. The mere arc of a boot heal on his side of the stream in *wet* mud.

Got him.

Adrenaline hit him in the gut and his pulse surged. Encouraged, Jack marked the track and searched for the next clue. He flipped the collar of his jacket up against the chill in the air and stepped out. His exertion kept the cold at bay. Ten feet more and Jack found a small patch of sand from the stream clumped on top of otherwise regular dark-brown dirt. Then he noticed a section of crushed leaves surrounded by a tapestry of undisturbed foliage.

His breath led the way in bursts of steam, and Jack's ears stung with cold. The mountain grade steepened, and made the going more difficult. Again, Jack wished he had been more prepared for this trek. They'd been in such a rush to start tracking that they weren't as properly rigged as they should have been. Ropes and a pickaxe would have been welcome tools on this incline. He tried the radio again, but still no response.

Fifteen feet had passed since the last indication that Hotchkiss had come through here, so Jack backtracked. He spiraled out from the last mark, searching for another. Though he wasn't certain, Jack found what might be a sign. It appeared as though there were two different tracks moving away from each other. Maybe Hotchkiss and the woman were together up to this point, or someone purposefully attempted to confuse the trail?

Jack employed the spiral search tactic once again, selecting the more prominent trail. He hiked for another mile before he found himself on the brink of a deep ravine.

Surely, Hotchkiss wouldn't have traversed down into the ravine. If he did, today's tracking ended. He didn't want to follow him down the cliff without the added safety of climbing gear Jack clenched his teeth together and let loose a frustrated growl. He stared hard at the ground hoping to see another mark.

Jack pulled water from his pack to moisten his dry throat. With his back to the cliff he gulped the clear liquid and then peered through the surrounding trees. A gray squirrel chittered at him from a tree branch above him. The lateness of the afternoon would soon force Jack to head back down to the compound. He certainly was not outfitted to camp overnight in the wilderness. The temperature already dipped below freezing and though his body stayed warm from his physical exertion, cold crept up his extremities.

Snap.

Jack's body went still. He focused on slowing his breathing to quiet his heart. Then he heard it again.

Crunch.

Human footfall or wildlife? Jack slid his fingers over the pistol grip of the gun in his shoulder holster. He crouched down and stared into the charged silence. He was exposed, out in the open with only the early gloaming for cover.

A loud pop resounded through the forest seconds before a slug rammed into Jack's chest. He heard a rifle report echo in the hills, half a second after the impact. Then instantly, two more slugs. He flew backward into the air, light as a feather. Air rushed from his lungs as a searing pain burst across his torso. He couldn't draw a breath. His vision dimmed. Jack reached his hands out to grasp onto something, anything. There was nothing.

Cold wind rushed around his head to his face. His lungs refused to pull in oxygen. Pain ignited throughout his body. His shoulder-blades slammed against something hard, immovable. His skull crashed into granite and the sharp tang of copper pressed into the back of his tongue. Agony exploded behind his eyes. Red. Yellow. White-hot light.

Then darkness stole him away.

CHAPTER 3

L aurel cringed at the gunshot echoing through the trees. Her horse, a big gorgeous paint, pranced nervously underneath her. "Steady, Wisaka."

Two more shots sounded and reverberated through her body. She watched the awkward ballet of the man's limbs as his wounded form flew into the air, through the canopy of trees, hitting branches on the way down to the ravine floor. Woodland birds screeched, wings fluttering amass, disturbed by his unexpected descent. Wisaka reared in fright, wanting to bolt, but Laurel held her firm. "Whoa, Wisaka. Steady, girl."

Laurel secured her rifle in its leather saddle-scabbard and pressed her horse into a lope as she rode down to the base of the cliff. She jumped from her mount, drew her rifle again, and peered up to the top of the ravine to see if anyone followed. Her heart hammered as she led her horse to cover. After waiting several minutes and not hearing or seeing anyone else,

Laurel tied Wisaka to a branch and crept toward the body. All the while keeping an eye on the ledge above.

She leveled her gun and stared down at the stranger. He looked as though he were merely having a sleep, with his dark lashes fanned across his cheekbones. She'd never seen this man around here before. He wore his almost black hair cut short on the sides and unlike the men she was accustomed to seeing every day, he shaved. A dark shadow of whiskers barely roughened his cheeks and jaw. She would have remembered seeing this face. He reminded her of a painting or a statue, and Laurel hesitated to touch him.

Laurel shook her head to clear the nonsense. She needed to focus on the task at hand. With another glance at the ridge above, Laurel reached her fingers under his square jaw and felt for a pulse in his neck.

She found a beat, and though it was weak, he still lived. She unzipped his jacket to assess his wounds and it surprised her not to see any blood. After further inspection, Laurel saw that the man wore a flak-jacket which had obviously saved his life.

Right—now what?

Strangers never came poking around here. Why did he? He should have been more careful. This was a dangerous place.

Laurel didn't have much time. Night crept along the ridge donning a cape of bitter wind. She tapped her lips with her fingers in indecision. In good conscience, she couldn't simply leave the bloke there. Since he was alive, she wanted to know who he was, and why he lurked about in the forest. He would surely die in the freeze overnight. She glanced around, assessing the available resources. Nodding to herself, she developed a plan. Before getting to work, Laurel took off her outer jacket and spread it over the unconscious man. Then, she returned to the trees to find Wisaka and the few tools she carried with her in her saddlebags.

First, Laurel attacked the base of a tall, young aspen tree with the serrated edge of her hunting knife. Once she was a little more than halfway through the trunk, she threw a rope up into the branches. After tying the other end of the rope to Wisaka's saddle horn, she guided her mare forward until the tree snapped off at the base, filling the air with the sharp, green scent of live wood. She repeated the process until she had two long, thin trees for the frame of a makeshift travois like the native people used over a hundred years ago.

She slid the aspen poles, one through each stirrup, before lashing them to the saddle with two long, leather concho-straps. Her cold fingers plucked at the ties on her blanket roll. Snapping it open, she secured the blanket with her rope like a sling between the two dragging ends of the trees, using the untrimmed branches as a sort of cushion. Laurel cut off any stray sticks that poked up into the blanket and then led Wisaka to where the man lay, still unconscious and crumpled in the dirt.

It took all her strength, and some she didn't know she had, to roll the stranger onto the travois. He was heavy—solid with no give. It crossed Laurel's mind briefly, that it might be dangerous to move him, but her only other option was to leave him, and he would certainly die if she did. She'd check him more thoroughly for wounds once they were safe inside a shelter, and figure out exactly who he was and what he wanted. Soft grunts and whimpering groans emitted from his throat when she pushed and pulled on his body. She hoped she wasn't causing him too much additional pain. With her final push, Laurel realized the back of his head was bleeding badly, so she wrapped her scarf tight around his skull and then pressed on.

When she had him on the sling, she covered him again. As she situated his outercoat, she felt something hard and smooth under his inner-liner. She lifted up the bottom edge and her eyes flew to the flashy gold FBI badge clipped to his waistband. Her hands moved faster than her mind and she felt for his firearm. She found it strapped to his side in a shoulder-holster. Laurel removed the gun and slipped it into the back of her own waistband. She stepped away and stared at the man. *An FBI agent. Bloody hell!*

Shaking her head, she removed his watch, utility belt, and radio, tossing them all in opposite directions. She opened his pack and emptied it out onto the musky mulch of the forest floor. Survival items along with a satellite phone, energy bars, and a bag of neon trail-flags dumped out, launching a plume of earth scented dust. She crushed the phone and radio with a stone the size of a rugby ball, pocketed the energy snacks, and rifled through the various other supplies.

Leaving the pack on the ground, she untied the man's boot laces and used them to secure his arms to the slender tree trunks so he wouldn't slide off. When Laurel was reasonably sure she had the agent anchored to the cot, and she wasn't taking anything with them that would reveal their location, she led Wisaka into the depths of the woods toward her cabin. She stopped every twenty feet for the first couple of miles to brush over the trail left on the decaying forest floor by the travois.

Darkness fell and Laurel traveled on by moonlight, rushing to find her little cabin deep in the woods. She would think about the consequences of saving this person—this FBI Agent—later. Just then, Laurel told herself, she didn't have the luxury or time for thinking.

***

Rick passed MacNeil off to the FBI intake team for processing before he went to the personnel-carrier to gather Jack's and his own cold weather gear. The temperature sank, and he had no time to waste.

"Sanchez," the SAC called from behind him. "Good work on finding MacNeil. No luck on Hotchkiss?"

"Not yet, sir. Stone is still on the mountain tracking him. I'm headed back out to join him now."

"I want you both back here by eighteen-thirty. It's too cold to be out past sunset. I've told the rest of the search team the same thing. If Hotchkiss is out there, he won't be going anywhere in the dark."

"Yes, sir. We'll do our best." Rick ducked into the van and located Jack's black gear-bag. He pulled out his partner's cold-weather gear and packed it along with his own. Next stop was the compound headquarters to load up on energy bars and water. He raced against the sun which was already hanging low in the sky.

Rick took an ATV to save time. He got to the rugged mountain trail in fifteen minutes and found

Jack's first fluorescent trail marker within the hour. He attempted radio contact several times, but got no response. Dusk snuck up on him as he drove along the edge of the stream. Rick came to a stop at the last trail marker. He focused on the ground, looking for signs of his partner's presence. His trail simply disappeared.

Rick stood and pulled out his night-vision binoculars. He scanned the terrain in all directions. A ravine fell away to his left and thick forest crowded in on all other sides, but he saw no sign of Jack.

"Where'd you go, man?" Rick said into the silent forest. He clicked on his radio and tried one more time. Snowflakes drifted softly across his face and he sighed. Frustration tightened the muscles in his jaw and neck. "Jack!" He yelled into the woods. "Jack!"

It wasn't like Jack to neglect leaving a marker, and Rick saw no sign of struggle. It looked like Jack stopped right on that spot. His boot prints suggested he turned and maybe squatted, and then nothing. Rick peered over the edge of the cliff for signs of his friend but there were none. It was as if they beamed him up to the mother ship. "Jack!" Rick called again.

Dark pressed full on now and Rick glanced at his watch. 20:00. "Damn." He knew he had to get to a spot where he could radio the compound. He was already an hour and a half late. The SAC would chew his ass, but he didn't want him sending out another search team.

He climbed onto the ATV and aimed its nose downhill. By the time he arrived at the half-way point, thick, heavy snow blew at an angle, blocking his vision as much as the sand-storms in the desert of Afghanistan. They couldn't possibly deploy a search team in this blinding snow. They'd have to wait for the storm to pass.

"Headquarters, come in." Rick paused on the trail. "Sanchez to Headquarters, come in."

"This is Headquarters. Sanchez, what's your twenty? Do you have Agent Stone?"

"Negative. Unable to locate Stone. I'm on my way in. ETA thirty-minutes."

"Confirm. You do *not* have Agent Stone?"

"Roger that. On my way. Be there in thirty. Out."

Rick's only consolation was Jack's knowledge and experience with wilderness survival tactics. If anyone could survive in a winter storm, it was Jack Stone. The pack he carried felt heavy with the gear he knew Jack needed and his gut tightened, shooting burning bile up his esophagus. "Shit." Rick revved the ATV and exhaust fumes clouded the pristine air.

He skidded to a halt in front of the headquarters building and sprinted up the steps. "We need a K-9 unit right away," he yelled as he ran through the doors.

"Calm down, Agent Sanchez. What happened out there? Where is Stone?"

"I can't explain it, sir." Rick stood before the SAC. "On the way up, Stone regularly left trail markers every twenty feet. His trail was easy to follow until it just stopped. There were no more markers, footprints, or signs of any kind. It's like he disappeared. We need a dog."

"And we'll take one up, but we can't do anything in this storm. We'll have to wait until morning."

"Sir, the temperature is dropping fast, and the snow is dumping. Stone is without his extreme cold weather gear."

"I presume he had his tactical pack with him?"

Rick nodded.

The SAC patted Rick's shoulder. "He has food, flint, and an emergency blanket. He can start a fire and he'll be able to survive."

"But sir—"

"Sorry, Sanchez. I cannot risk more agents in this storm. Let's trust Stone to do what we both know he can do, and we'll go out again in the morning, with the dogs."

"Sir—"

"Stand down, Sanchez. Get dinner and some sleep. I need you to lead the team out first thing in the morning."

***

Two and a half hours of hard travel later, Wisaka pulled the injured agent into the small cabin's clearing. By then, it was full-on dark, and what had started out as a sifting of snowflakes became a dense curtain of white. Grateful she had banked the embers in the stone fireplace before she left, Laurel looked forward to the warmth of the one-room cabin. But first, she had a more immediate challenge she hadn't considered.

The man she had literally dragged home was far too heavy for her to lift. She hopped down from the saddle and stood at the side of the travois considering her options. Laurel wrapped her arms around herself and stamped her feet, chasing off the chill. She shuddered with apprehension at the mess she'd gotten herself into this time, but it was too late now. She could never leave an injured animal to suffer to death in the forest and a man was no different.

Now, to get him inside. Laurel untied the poles and walked Wisaka forward, letting the posts slide out from the stirrups. She went into the small barn attached to the rear of the cabin and retrieved another long rope. Tying the pole ends together, she uncoiled the rope as she went inside. She stopped to place two logs on the hot embers and they rewarded her with an immediate combustion and the warm, tangy scent of burning pine. Laurel crossed the room and opened a window on the back wall of the cabin. Tossing the rest of the rope through the opening, she jogged out to get her horse.

She paused to check on the man. He was breathing but was still unconscious and she felt his weak pulse. "Hold on, mister. I'll have you inside in a jiff."

Laurel led her horse to the back side of the cabin and tied the rope she passed through the window onto her saddle horn. Slowly, she urged Wisaka to pull the weight attached to the rope. Her plan worked, and though the trees got caught on the door frame and made the ride a bumpy one that crumbled leaves and sticks across the floor, the horse dragged the pallet inside. Watching through the window at her progression, she stopped her horse when the travois lay in front of the fireplace.

Laurel tossed the rope in through the window and shut it against the freeze. She ran back inside and placed another log onto the fire to banish the cold air from the room. Before she went out to put Wisaka away in her stall, she covered the man with a thick quilt.

When her father built the cabin, he included a

small stall with room for hay and tack. A short, enclosed walkway attached the tiny barn and the cabin so when the weather turned bad, she wouldn't have to go outside to tend to her horse. Laurel was once again thankful for the indoor connection with the winter storm coming in. She threw some hay to Wisaka and rushed into the main cabin through the passageway.

The agent's sallow and pale face stood in stark contrast to his dark hair. Laurel filled a kettle with water from a barrel and hung it over the fire to heat. She knelt beside him, and as gently as she could, unwrapped her scarf from his head. A good amount of copper-scented blood soaked the wool, but the gash clotted over and no new blood seeped out. Laurel moved to assess his other injuries. She thought for certain the bullets hit him, but she hadn't seen any blood on his clothing.

She folded the blanket down and removed the coat she'd covered him with. After unzipping his jacket, she ran her fingers over the man's Kevlar body-armor. Three rifle slugs sat imbedded in the heavy vest. One nestled right over his heart. "Lucky for you, you weren't shot in the head," she murmured.

The clasps on the vest were tight and Laurel tore a fingernail below the skin trying to undo them. She sucked her finger before trying again to remove his protective gear. She lifted the hem of his shirt to see what damage the shots had caused. Deep blue and purple bruising mottled his muscled chest. Laurel slid her knife from the scabbard on her belt and cut his camouflage Under Armour shirt away. She drew a sharp breath at the sight of the full damage apparent on the man's torso.

"Sure and those ribs might be broken," she said to the agent. She glanced up, to see if he remained unconscious. Never having been this close to a man's bare chest before, she tentatively stretched out her fingers to touch him. He was hard, not like some of the flabby men she had seen at a distance on the compound. But he wasn't bony like the younger ones either. This man's chest and belly were firm and well defined. She pushed gently along his ribs, checking for serious breaks. Her fingers itched to touch him and her pulse danced. Then, like a naughty child, she let her fingers glide over the soft black hair on his chest.

Her cheeks burned, and she snatched her hand away.

Steam rolled out of the kettle's spout and she swung it away from the flames on its hook. She poured boiling water into a bowl, added some cold water to cool it, and dunked in a wash flannel. Tenderly, she blotted the drying blood from the man's head. When she finished cleaning his wound, she bandaged the injury with supplies from her first-aid kit and gently laid his head onto a pillow.

She pulled off his boots and felt his legs and ankles for broken bones. No sharp angles alarmed her, so she concentrated her efforts on tending to his ribs. She couldn't do much, even if his ribs were cracked, other than lay strips of frozen cloths on the bruises.

To prevent him from getting chilled, she kept the fire blazing. She dunked rags into cold water to hang outside over the rail where they would freeze. Her eyes widened when she stepped out on the porch and saw four inches of snow already covering the ground.

She counted it as good luck because she could use the snow to help keep any swelling down.

Laurel filled an oilskin bag with snow to create a makeshift ice-pack for her patient's head. After tending to him and assuring herself he was warm enough, she sat down for a simple tea of beans on toast. The savory sauce of the beans warmed her from within. But she'd have to go out hunting again tomorrow since she didn't get any meat today. She hardly had any left in the cellar and they couldn't survive on beans alone.

After she cleaned up her meal, Laurel found her sketchbook and a piece of charcoal. She sat on the bed, leaning against the cabin wall and stared at the man. She wanted to recreate the peaceful way his lashes rested against his skin, the way they made this grown man look young and vulnerable. Her hand began to move with short arcing motions. The charcoal made a gratifying scratching sound against the drawing paper as his form took shape.

Laurel startled from her drawing when the man mumbled something in his sleep. She couldn't make out his words, but she watched him from the bed and wondered what would happen when he woke up. *Why was an FBI Agent wandering around the mountains by himself? It was a dangerous part of the country for lawmen. Any of us living on the compound who saw him snooping around would be expected to shoot him on sight.*

Suddenly nervous about him waking up, Laurel used his boot laces to re-tie his wrists to the aspen poles of his cot. If he did wake up, she'd be prepared. Her da always told her not to trust the FBI. She found some twine and lashed the agent's ankles to the poles too, for good measure.

Before she turned in for the night, Laurel slid her sketchbook back into the dresser drawer and went to collect one more round of frozen cloths to put on the agent's bruised ribs. When she stepped outside to get the fresh strips, the snow was more than a foot deep and she had to shake the cloths out. Back inside, she knelt next to her patient, bending to her work. She glanced at his features for the hundredth time, drawn by the cut of his cheekbones and his strong jaw as much as by the black whiskers dusting across his pale skin. In his sleep, she could see the lad he had once been. She lifted her fingers to touch his cheek when the man's hand jerked, and though his arm strained against the ties, his fingers clamped painfully onto her wrist. Her heart leapt to the top of her throat. Bright-blue eyes snapped open and bored into her.

CHAPTER 4

"Who the hell are you?" Jack demanded.

The woman stifled a scream. Her green eyes flashed with fright.

He glared at her. "Where am I?" He cringed against a brutal pain stabbing his lungs when he breathed and struggled to speak.

The woman regained her composure and stared down at him. "You're in my cabin."

Jack narrowed his eyes at the woman. He gingerly took a breath. "Why?" He tried to move and when he couldn't, he growled. "Why am I tied down?"

The woman lifted her chin and looked down the slope of her nose. "In case you're dangerous. I wanted to be prepared." She twisted her arm out of his grasp and her fingers flew to a silver charm hanging at her neck. He exerted too much effort asking his questions and he couldn't hold on to her. His head throbbed and exhaustion pressed down on him.

Jack looked down. His chest lay bare except for four or five strips of cold cloth. He scrunched his brow at the bruises splayed across his skin. His head pounded and his chest burned.

In a softer voice he asked, "What happened?"

The woman stood and moved away from him. She sat in a chair at the small table across the room. "You were shot."

Jack closed his eyes trying to recall. He remembered tracking Hotchkiss. Then it all came swirling back. Something that felt like a truck had slammed into his chest.

"Who are you?" Jack tried to place her soft accent when she spoke.

The woman cocked her head to the side and said nothing for a long moment. Finally, side-stepping his questions, she said, "You're FBI. What are you doing up here?" The woman's eyes narrowed with distrust.

Jack glanced around the one-room cabin. He lay bound next to a stone fireplace, and observed the only light in the shelter came from the warm blaze and two lanterns. On the far wall stood a coal-burning stove and a sink with a red water-pump mounted on the counter next to it. Rustic. He noted one exterior door, an interior door, and three windows—two at the front and one in the rear. All possible exits. He registered one rifle leaned up against the wall by the front door. His pulse kicked.

"Did *you* shoot me?"

The woman leveled her gaze at him and then rose and walked to the front window. "We're getting a ton of snow. It's a good thing I didn't leave you out there. You'd have frozen to death." As if to add emphasis to her words a lone wolf howled in the distance.

"Where's my pack? My gun?" Jack's mind tumbled through his thoughts. None of this made any sense. His vision swam and his body released its tension. He couldn't keep his eyes open.

At some later point, he became vaguely aware of a beautiful woman laying a blanket over him. He wanted to thank her, but he drifted away on dark waves of slumber.

***

Laurel could not fall asleep with an FBI agent laying on her floor. She rubbed her tender wrist where he'd grabbed her, stunned by his strength even in a barely-conscious state. She wouldn't make the mistake of getting that close again. Maybe the FBI finally discovered the compound. If so, she was glad she wasn't down there at the time.

Her mind waffled between wondering why the man was there and wanting to study him while he slept. Outside, snow swirled against the cabin, coming down so thick she couldn't see farther than a few inches out the window. The last time she went out for wood, she carried in all the logs stacked on the porch. They'd have enough to keep them warm for a day, maybe two, before she'd have to take the sled out to the woodshed to get more. By then she might have to dig her way out the front door.

Wisaka whinnied from the stable and Laurel slipped on a pair of wellies and a jacket to go feed her mare. The mercury fell when she stepped into the short hallway. On her way to the stall, Laurel pulled a horse blanket from the rack. She threw it over Wisaka's back and withers and buckled the straps. She tossed two flakes of hay into the feed-bin and gave her horse a scoop of grain. After stroking the horse's nose, Laurel hurried back inside the cabin.

The agent still slept. He seemed peaceful, though bruised and hurting. The man looked like someone she would want to know. *But, appearances are often deceiving.* Laurel knelt next to him and felt his brow for fever with the back of her hand. His skin was hot. She turned her hand over and rested her palm on the side of his cheek. *Low-grade fever.* She briefly cupped his face, wondering about him. *Who is he? Does he have a family fretting about him tonight?*

Laurel shook her head at her own daftness, yet even as she stood she couldn't help but glance at his left hand. *No ring.* "Which means absolutely nothing—and who cares, anyway? Oi! What is the matter with me?" Her voice echoed loud in the quiet cabin where the only other sounds were the crackling fire and an occasional soft snore from the man on the floor.

Laurel swung the kettle on its hook over the flames to heat water for a cup of tea. She snuggled up in her blankets at the corner of the bed and sat up watching the man's chest rise and fall with his breath, wondering if the simple life-sustaining movement caused him terrible pain.

In the subdued early light, Laurel rubbed her eyes to clear them. It was utterly silent and too dark for this time of the morning. She pulled aside the red and black flannel curtain to see a wall of snow drifted up against the window insulating the cabin from any outdoor sounds. Laurel scooted off the bed and inspected the other windows, finding more of the same. The accumulation averaged over four feet high and it was still snowing. At this rate, it wouldn't be long before they were completely snowed in.

Thankful she had brought in all the firewood the previous night, Laurel poked at the embers in the fireplace and placed two more logs on top to build the flame back up. Her patient slept. She wasn't sure if sleeping was safe with a concussion or not, but she didn't think she could wake him even if she tried. Laurel touched his face and her brows knit. He was still feverish. He needed another snow pack on his head wound.

His startling blue eyes snapped opened and stared at her.

"Good morning," she said, fisting her hands then wiping them on her jeans.

He continued to stare at her, contemplating. "Where am I?"

"In my cabin."

A small, impatient breath rushed out through his nose. "And, where is *that*?"

"Idaho."

The man closed his eyes. He shifted his weight and groaned. His biceps strained against the restraints on his arms. Anger flared in his eyes when they flew open again. "Untie me."

"Not bloody likely." Laurel backed away from him and tightened the blanket she had wrapped around her shoulders. "How are you feeling? Do you have any appetite?"

The man's dark eyebrows scrunched together as if he couldn't understand her words.

"Who are you?" he growled.

"Who are *you*?"

"Can we please stop playing word games? My head is killing me. Tell me what the hell is going on."

"We had a blizzard last night and we're just about snowed in." Laurel opened the front door to a wall of snow three-fourths the way up the opening and her jaw dropped. "Bugger. I'll have to get out to the woodshed and fetch more logs in, while I still can." She turned to see his reaction.

He laid back and shut his eyes and the muscles in his jaw rippled against his pain.

"You need a cold pack for the swelling on your head. You cracked it good on a rock after tumbling about twenty feet." Laurel grabbed a pot and scooped it full of snow. After setting it on a burner, she started a small fire in the ancient cast-iron stove to heat it. "I'll make some porridge for breakfast. If your stomach is queasy, it might help you feel better."

Laurel refilled the oilskin bag with snow and lifted the man's head so he could rest it on the cold. He grimaced at the movement, then settled back.

"You're going to have to untie me. I have to pee." He pulled lightly against the laces holding his wrist. "Don't tell me you have an outhouse."

She smiled. "No. Luckily, there's a pit-toilet on the other side of the barn."

Again the man looked at her like she spoke a foreign language. Then she realized he didn't know her barn was accessible from the cabin. She explained.

"So… untie me."

The water on the stove bubbled. Laurel poured in the oats and stirring, she turned down the heat. The homey actions gave her time to think. Nerves pranced along her breastbone. He was awake and she had to deal with him.

"Right—I'll untie you. But I have your gun, and I know well how to use it. So don't try anything." She found his handgun and slid it in the waistband of her jeans before she moved to the rifle propped by the door. Laurel lifted her firearm and opened the chamber, emptying the bullets out. She stuffed them into her pocket.

With a flick of her knife, she released one of his wrists and then moved away. She retrieved his gun and pointed it at him while he untied his other wrist and then strained to undo his ankles. He rested a moment before he attempted to stand. Agony pinched his face into a grimace when he tried to sit up. He rolled to his side and groaned.

He breathed heavily. "I need help."

Laurel hesitated. She hated seeing anyone in so much pain, but he was a potential enemy. She knew nothing about him, really. He could hurt her and there was no one around to back her up or hear her scream.

"Please." The word floated out on a desperate whisper.

She rolled her lower lip between her front teeth. But in the end, she wasn't keen to stand there and watch the man suffer. Laurel released the magazine from the handgun and hid the parts separately in the kitchen. "Okay, I'll help you, but don't try anything. In your condition, I could hurt you."

The man nodded and when he did, blood oozed from his head wound again. He needed water and a bandage wrapped around his cut. She would do that when he returned. For now, Laurel slid her hands under his arms and helped him get to his knees.

"At first I thought your ribs were broken, but

they might just be cracked where the bullets impacted your Kevlar-vest."

"I was shot?" His hand touched his injured ribs.

Laurel nodded, watching him try to assimilate the information. The concussion likely caused memory issues.

Drips of sweat popped out along his hairline and he tried to take a deep breath. "Okay, ready?" He forced one knee forward and got a foot on the floor before he rested again. Another breath, this one shallower. "Let's do this." He leaned his weight into Laurel and she fought to support him as he stood.

With the arm closest to her, he clutched Laurel's wrist and spun her so fast it disoriented her. Before she registered what was happening, he had her arm twisted up behind her and held one of his across her throat. Blood surged through her veins, adrenaline giving her power. Laurel kicked at his legs, but he'd set them wide apart so she couldn't reach him. She bucked against his chest, hoping to hurt him bad enough he would have to let go.

He cried out, but held fast. She threw her head backward to ram his nose but couldn't find her target. He pinned her arms against her body. Surprised by his strength even though he was injured, she struggled with all of her might to get free. She kicked her legs frantically, forcing him to bear her full weight. Laurel tried to bite him, but he held her jaw in the vice of his elbow. He had her in a choke hold. Dark mist seeped in around her vision.

She had seconds, at best.

Bastard.

***

Rick rose before dawn. He repacked his gear along with Jack's. By 06:30 he strode into the makeshift mess hall to recruit the best trackers for his search and rescue team. Four men plus a female agent and her K-9 partner geared up for the early morning trek. Rick explained how Jack's trail had simply come to a halt.

The dog handler approached him, her bloodhound at her heel on his tether. The trim, serious woman thrust out her hand toward Rick. "I'm Agent Kendra Dean. I am with the Hostage Rescue Team, K9 Division, out of Denver. Your SAC requested our assistance."

Rick shook her hand while assessing her. She'd pinned her thick brown hair into a severe military-style bun at the nape of her neck. She wore no make-up on her amber eyes, which stared directly into Rick's. "Thanks for coming. We have an agent missing on the mountain. We lost contact with him yesterday around 16:00. He may be injured. We need all hands on deck doing what we can to find him." He handed the K-9 agent a shirt from Jack's bag.

The dog handler drew the side of her mouth back and shrugged. "We'll try, but it snowed a couple of feet last night. I can't promise Baxter here will be able to pick up a scent through the accumulation."

"He's got to." Rick crossed his arms.

She knelt by her dog and let him smell the shirt. "We'll do the best we can."

Rick glared at her. Excuses wouldn't get Jack back home safe. "Where's the medic? Do we have a toboggan in case Jack's injured?"

"We're locked and cocked," one of the men

responded.

"Good. Let's go."

The team assembled outside and mounted four-wheel drive ATV's. Rick gave a general description of the trail they were taking before he hopped on his rig and drove out the rear compound gate. The team struggled to climb the mountain for about a mile before it became obvious the ATV's weren't the vehicles for the job. Even with the four-wheel drive, they couldn't make it through the deep, freshly fallen snow. Icy winds whipped around the agents, blasting frozen crystals into their faces. Visibility was about ten feet. The weather forced the team to turn back. Rick wondered how long it would take for a fleet of snowmobiles to arrive.

He stomped his boots before entering the temporary headquarters, and stood before the SAC. "The official search will have to wait until we can get snowmobiles up here." Rick perched his hands on his hips. "But I'm going out again this morning. I'll go on foot."

"Use your head, Sanchez. You won't be able to find any tracks. Our only hope at this point is the dog, and he needs the snowmobile to get up there."

"I can't sit here and do nothing. Stone could be hurt. Every minute counts. He already had to survive through the night."

The SAC stood behind his desk. "The last thing I need is for you to get lost in this blizzard too. I can't afford to lose any more agents. No one goes out there until we have the correct gear. Is that clear?"

Rick stared at his commander. "Yes, sir."

"I have to call Stone's family and let them know he's missing. You two are friends, do you know his family?" The SAC sat back in his chair.

Rick gave his commander a curt nod. "I'd like to make the call, sir."

"You sure?"

"Yes, sir. Jack and I are close." Rick turned to go, then hesitated. "Jack's brother is getting married tomorrow. He hoped to be home for the wedding." He rubbed a hand over his face. "Can I wait until after we send the search team out? I don't want to alarm Jack's family unnecessarily. I'd rather call with the news that he's okay."

His commander's eyes softened, and he nodded. "It's best to call right away, but I suppose you can wait until tomorrow morning. Let's see if Jack makes it back here tonight. If I know Jack, there's a good possibility he will."

Rick briefly closed his eyes, shutting down thoughts of Jack out in the blizzard with no cold weather gear. "God, I hope so."

"Thanks, Sanchez. Get some rest."

"Roger that." Rick stepped out on the front porch, flipping through his contacts. Jack and he had exchanged family contact information, just in case. He located a number for Caedon Stone, Jack's oldest brother. This was not the way he wanted to meet Jack's family. God, he hoped he could call them with good news.

CHAPTER 5

Wildcat. Jack eased the woman down onto the bed. He took a few precious seconds to pant through the pain that threatened his own consciousness. Then, using the same laces she'd tied him with, he bound her wrists together behind her back. He used twine to tie her feet to the foot of the bedframe.

Oatmeal boiled over the side of the pot in the kitchen and Jack inched his way to the stove and took it off the heat. His brain throbbed. He found a bucket with water and a ladle. He dipped it in and drank deeply. Breathing was a feat, so he took a minute to concentrate simply on that before he searched for his SIG Sauer and its magazine. He gave himself five minutes to get a grip before he stumbled through the door to the other side of the barn to use the head.

The cold air in the stall was balm to his fevered body. Jack leaned against the wall and fought to remember what happened to him in the wilderness, his memory fuzzy around the edges. He'd been tracking Jedediah Hotchkiss when he heard a sound. Then he was hit. The searing pain he experienced when the bullet impacted his body-armor gave him a new appreciation for his brother, Trent, who was shot in the shoulder by one of these Nazi terrorists several weeks ago in Flint River.

Someone had leaked information about a school bombing and prevented the deaths of hundreds of children. But the bomber, Eugene Werner, escaped, and Jack tracked him into the mountains above Flint River. Before they caught him, the bastard murdered Matthew Jefferson, a close friend of Trent's, and in the process of apprehending him, Trent took a bullet. The whole situation had turned into a shit-storm, and Jack prayed Trent was gaining some peace after the loss of his friend. Eventually Werner had given the Feds the location of the compound in Idaho filled with like-minded believers in exchange for a plea deal. His trial was currently taking place in the 7th District Federal Court in Chicago. Jack had given a deposition and may still be called in to testify.

Jack remained in the cold with the woman's horse while he considered his injuries. His legs felt bruised, but nothing too bad—no breaks or sprains that he could detect. He agreed with his captive that his ribs probably weren't broken, but they sure hurt like hell. Each bone burned like a welding torch when he moved. He figured he had a concussion, but that would heal with time. And they had plenty of that with a blizzard snowing them in.

His next thought hit him like a bulldozer. *Sanchez will never be able to track me with all this snow. They'll think I'm dead.*

Jack took small breaths as he made his way

through the passage into the cabin. The fire burned hot, warming the room, but it didn't hold anywhere near the heat as the green eyes that glared at him when he came through the door.

"Are you okay?" he asked.

"I can't believe I trusted you. My da always said not to trust the law. I should have known."

Jack shrugged but winced at the movement. "Criminals definitely should beware of the law. That much is true." He shuffled into the kitchen and found some bowls. "You want breakfast?"

The woman wrestled against her restraints but other than offering a growl of frustration, she didn't answer him. She radiated defiance and in her rage she was breathtaking. Her long black hair fanned across the pillow and tangled around her face.

"No?" Jack casually spooned the hot cereal into his bowl and banged the ladle on the edge of the pot. He carried his breakfast to the table and sat gingerly. "What's your name?"

She glared.

"Come on. It's not a crucial piece of top-secret information." He swallowed a bite and closed his eyes, enjoying the soothing warm cereal as it slid down his throat. "I'm Jack. Jack Stone."

"*Special Agent*, Jack Stone," she spit.

"Yeah, that's true, but irrelevant in this situation, I think. Tell me your name."

She sighed, seemingly defeated. "Laurel MacNeil."

Jack forced his face to remain passive as his mind leapt to attention. *MacNeil? The daughter of the man second in command of the neo-Nazi militia?* "Nice to meet you, Laurel," he kept his tone level.

Bottle-green eyes spewed venom and fury in

response.

"Why'd you shoot me?" He ate another bite. "You couldn't have known I was FBI. Do you usually shoot random strangers?"

"I did'na bloody-well shoot you."

Jack considered the faint lilt in her words. *Irish? Scottish, maybe?* "No? Then who did?"

"How would I know?"

"You were obviously there."

Laurel turned her face to the wall. Jack finished his bland cereal and put the bowl in the dishpan. He scooped a ladle of cold water in it to soak. "Do you want me to bring you some oatmeal?" He tried again. The woman didn't answer, so he nudged a chair over next to the bed with this foot and sat.

She glanced at him from under long strands of her hair which she shook and tried to blow from her face. "You need to bandage your head. Your wound is seeping. You also should put an ice-pack on it to keep the swelling down."

"Thanks." Jack laughed. "You're spitting mad, but you still care about my wounds?"

"I'm not a barbarian."

"No, you just live with them?"

Laurel gave him a look he couldn't interpret. "Will you untie my hands so I can eat?"

Jack cocked his head and considered the beautiful handful in front of him. "I suppose I could do that. Only your hands though, and I *am* armed."

She rolled her eyes. "Aye, fine."

Jack steeled himself against the pain of moving and went to dish her up a bowl of oatmeal.

Laurel watched him. "Butter and sugar, please. They're on the counter."

Jack's lips curled on one side and he added the requested flavors. He untied her hands and then moved his chair to sit across the room from her with his gun out on the table next to him.

"If you didn't shoot me, who did?"

Laurel ignored him and pretended the oatmeal fascinated her.

"Was it Hotchkiss? Do you know where he is?" He tried again.

"Is that who you were chasing about in the woods?"

"Yes."

"Then probably. I honestly did'na see who shot you. I heard the gunshots and then saw you fall off the ledge at the ravine." Laurel set her bowl on the nightstand and pulled pillows behind her so she could lean on them against the wall. "No one came to finish the job, so I brought you here."

"How did you do that—all by yourself?" Jack scoffed.

Laurel stared at him. "I wasn't by myself. I have a horse. We dragged you here."

"You want me to believe you selflessly saved my life? Me? An FBI Agent?"

"I'm not a murderer."

"No?" A hot ire ignited behind Jack's sternum. "Everyone who lives in your compound is culpable for the murder of two Chicago police officers. And what about the kids at the school Werner tried to blow up? I want to know the real reason you brought me here."

The blood drained from Laurel's face. "I— But the bombing never happened, though." Her eyes flashed.

"Thank God." Jack leaned his head back. His elevated blood pressure exacerbated the stabbing pain in his skull. "But that's not enough. You're all going down for domestic terrorism."

"But—" Laurel's eyes were wide. She swallowed and licked her lips. "I rang the police."

Jack sat forward and gasped. He took several breaths as sharp blades scraped along his ribcage. He focused intently on her. "What do you mean, *you rang?*"

"I rang in an anonymous tip." Her gaze fell to her lap, and a tear hovered at the corner of her eye. "What ended up happening to Eugene?"

Staring at Laurel, Jack's eyes narrowed at her statement. *Laurel called in the anonymous tip?* None of this made sense. He pulled his lower lip through his teeth as he considered what he should say.

"Jedediah Hotchkiss, your illustrious leader, abandoned Werner after they arrested him for the failed bombing attempt in Chicago. A mere hour after Werner realized they'd hung him out to dry, the scumbag started singing for a plea deal." Jack squeezed his temples between his thumb and middle finger to relieve his pounding head. "He gave the FBI the exact location of your hidden militia compound. That neo-Nazi piss-ant told us where to look, gave us the number of occupants, and the compound layout. He sold all of you out."

"Did he tell you there were little kids living there?" Laurel's eyes swam with concern.

Jack nodded and cocked his head. "*You* called in the tip?"

Laurel released a pent-up breath. "Yes," she answered. "They're all right, then? The children are safe?"

"Yeah, don't worry. We were particularly careful, knowing they were present."

"So, what happens to Eugene now?"

"Werner was indicted on four counts of murder and conspiracy by bombing, domestic terrorism, and a federal hate crime charge, including the use of a firearm to commit murder. He escaped the federal death penalty with his plea deal. Bargained for a reduced sentence of three consecutive life sentences." Jack adjusted his position and measured his breath. "He'll live the rest of his life inside a federal supermax." He smirked. Jack had no doubt the asshole would get what he deserved on the inside.

"He won't likely live to the end of a life sentence. Jedediah is connected with neo-Nazi gangs in the prison systems."

"No, he probably won't." Jack watched the emotions storming in Laurel's eyes and across her face. "Does that bother you? Did you have feelings for Werner?"

"God, no."

"Then why are you upset? If you're the one who tipped off the Feds, you saved hundreds of lives. *Children's* lives." Jack tried to stand but his head swam so he sat back down.

"I'm not upset about telling the police. I'm sad for so many other reasons. The whole bloody situation." Laurel wiped her face on her shoulder and narrowed her eyes at him. "Listen, Agent Stone, you ought to be in hospital. Since that's not possible, you must lie down." She reached forward, keeping her focus on his gun. When she moved to untie her feet, he didn't try to stop her.

Laurel stood and crossed the room with her empty bowl, stacking it on top of his. Jack followed her movements from the corner of his eye. He'd see her coming if she tried to attack him, but honestly, he didn't think he had the strength to ward her off again.

"Come on, let me help you lay down on the bed. You need rest." She pushed her hands under his arms and helped him stand.

"I got it." Jack pushed through the pain and walked on his own, hoping to hide the truth of his weakness.

"Fine." She stepped away and watched him ease himself onto the bed. He groaned when his head pressed into the pillow. "Right. I'll bring in some snow and find a roll of cotton-wool for your head."

"Don't try anything stupid," he said through gritted teeth. He squeezed his eyelids shut against the hot poker that jabbed at his brain.

"It's not as though either one of us is going anywhere in the immediate future."

Jack watched her through almost closed eyelids. She poured warm water from the kettle into a bowl and dropped a cloth into it. On a tray, she set the bowl, a bottle of Betadine, and the bandage roll, then she carried her supplies to the bedside table next to him.

"Can you roll to the side? I'll clean the cut on your head and get you plastered up."

Jack didn't like the idea of putting his back to her, but he figured if she wanted him dead, she wouldn't have gone to the effort of saving him.

The woman pressed a warm, wet cloth to his head, blotting his wound. Water and the antiseptic stung like hell, but once he was bandaged and resting on the snow-filled oilcloth, he felt better than he had all morning.

"I don't have any heavy-duty pain medicine, but I do have Tylenol. Fancy some?"

"Yeah, that'd be great." He reached for her arm. "Thanks, Laurel."

She stilled and held his gaze with her remarkable sea-storm eyes for a long moment, as though she sought to figure him out. Then she shrugged and picked up her tray. "It's nae bother."

Jack watched her working in the kitchen for a few minutes before he drifted off to sleep.

The sound of a rifle shot jolted him awake. His body instinctively prepared to take cover before he remembered it hurt to move. "Ahh!" He eased himself into the pillow and waited for his pulse to settle and the pain to subside.

"Nightmare?" Laurel looked up from a book she held in her lap. She sat curled up in an old plaid armchair, in front of the fire.

"I guess."

She offered him a sympathetic frown. "Hungry?"

Jack's stomach rumbled in response to the suggestion. The side of his mouth quirked up. "Apparently so."

"You slept through lunch. Dinner will be ready in a wee bit. I'll bring you some crackers to hold you over."

Jack had a hard time reconciling this woman's compassion and gentle manner with a woman who held neo-Nazi beliefs and lived her life among those who would gladly kill people who were different from them. She brought him a plate of crackers with slices of cheddar cheese and a glass of cold water.

"Thanks."

"You never told me why you were up in the mountains tracking Jed. He almost never comes up here to the wilderness." She pulled a kitchen chair over to his bedside.

"The FBI invaded your compound, but you, Hotchkiss and MacNeil escaped." Jack nibbled on a cracker, the snack settling his queasy stomach.

"I didn't escape, I didn't even know you took over the compound."

"How did you get out? No one saw you."

Laurel shrugged. "I rode my horse. And to be fair, I didn't see anyone either. The forest is thick on that side of the valley."

"Who is Roger MacNeil to you? You have the same last name. Is he your father?"

Laurel nodded, but didn't speak. She looked away and stared at the fire.

"My partner caught up to him yesterday. He captured your dad and took him down to headquarters. He was coming back to help hunt down Hotchkiss."

She nodded again and slowly turned to face Jack. "Did anyone get hurt when you took over the camp?"

Jack ignored her questions, too filled with his own. "What are you doing with this group, Laurel? Do you really believe you're better than others just because the color of your skin?"

Her eyes hardened like cut glass. "Of course not." She stood and walked to the fire, her arms crossed in front of her as she stared at the flame. "I'm only here because my father forced me to live here with him when I was sixteen." She shoved her fingers into the hair at her temples. "I hate their beliefs." Laurel turned to Jack. "But I don't have anywhere else to go."

"Bullshit." Jack felt a little stronger with food in his belly. He pushed himself up to sit against the headboard. "You're what, twenty-five, twenty-six? I'm not buying."

Laurel scrunched her brows and lifted her chin. "You wouldn't understand." She went to the kitchen and opened the oven door. A savory, comforting aroma drifted across the room. Jack's mouth watered and his stomach tightened in anticipation.

She scooped some of the appetizing dish into a bowl and brought it to him. "Where am I supposed to go? I have no ID, no money…"

He reached for the food—a thick stew with a flaky crust on top—and he breathed in the gravy-scented steam. "Nope. Still not buying it. You could have gone to the police right away. They would have helped you."

"I *did* go to the police. I rang them and told them about the bombing." Laurel spun toward the kitchen to dish up her own dinner. "I had to steal my da's mobile. He almost caught me, and I had to return it. If Jedediah found out I snitched, I would be dead."

"Okay, so you made the call. But that doesn't explain why you've stayed on the compound all these years if you didn't agree with their philosophy." Jack spooned a bite into his mouth and closed his eyes. *Delicious.* "Is this venison?"

Laurel's brow creased, and she seemed momentarily confused by the sudden change in subject. "Yes. I think we'll have enough to last us if we can dig out soon. I'd been hunting the day I found you, but didn't get anything." She took a bite of her meat pie and pressed her lips together. "This was my mam's recipe. Only she used mutton."

"It's really good." Jack scooped another spoonful. "Where is your mom?"

Laurel set her spoon on the table and cleared her throat. "Scotland."

"Scotland?" He regarded her. "I thought I detected an accent. Did you live there with her?"

Her smile was wistful and she took on a faraway gaze. "Yeah. I grew up in a small village in Perthshire, near Pitlochry." Laurel rotated her spoon in her fingers. "I miss her terribly."

"Why are you here then? If you have family— your mother—somewhere else, it doesn't make sense. You could have called her."

Laurel collected their dishes and carried them to the washtub. She pumped water into the sink and added hot water from the kettle. She washed and dried the dishes and tidied up the one-room cabin. "I need to feed Saka. Then, I'll tell you my story."

***

Rick gripped his phone so hard he thought he'd break it. "Yes, I understand. You can count on me to do everything humanly possible to find Jack."

Cade Stone barked orders through the line as though he and Rick were both still active duty Marines. "Our brother, Trent is getting married this evening. I won't tell him about Jack until after the ceremony, but you can be damn sure we'll be on the road to Idaho first thing. I expect to see Jack safe and sound when I get there. Do I make myself clear?"

"Yes, sir." Rick understood, but he wasn't sure he could follow Cade's order. The storm was only getting worse. "The team is leaving right now to start the search. We had to wait for snowmobiles, but we are ready to go now."

"Text me the GPS coordinates of the compound and then *find my brother*."

"Yes, sir." Rick ended the call and quickly pinged Cade his current location.

He went outside and approached the rescue team. They were securing their gear to the recently-arrived snowmobiles and had rigged one of them with a toboggan and first-aid supplies. Rick tried not to think of Jack laying somewhere, injured and freezing, or… He snapped his mind to the task at hand.

"Mount up. Let's go." Rick swung his leg over the seat of the first snowmobile and revved the engine. He moved out, followed by his team.

The K-9 officer's bloodhound rode in a kennel on a sled behind her and seemed unruffled by traveling in the unusual manner. His handler drove smoothly as she followed, not zipping forward like the other agents who sped up the trail, and ended up fishtailing.

Deep snow covered the markers Jack left along the trail, but Rick remembered where it was. Of course, the world looked different when covered in a blanket of snow. Especially when the blanket was two to three feet deep. He led the unit up the mountainside. They found the stream and followed it up to where Rick estimated Jack left its banks and headed north-west. Finally, they came to the edge of the chasm where Rick lost Jack's trail the day before.

"This is the location of Stone's last identifiable tracks." Rick untied a shovel from his sled and started to dig down. "Agent Dean, bring your dog."

The officer leashed her dog and approached him. "It's one thing to track in the snow, if there are fresh tracks, Sanchez, but Baxter won't be able to sniff out a trail left on the ground and then covered with two feet of snow."

"He can try." Rick knew it was unfair to expect miracles from the dog, but they needed one

The officer's expression softened with compassion. "I get it. Agent Stone is your partner." Kendra bent down and held Jack's shirt to Baxter's nose. "We'll try, of course. I just don't want you to have unrealistic expectations of my canine partner."

The dog sniffed the shirt and then stuck his nose in the snow. He pulled his muzzle out and shook his head, ears flopping, to remove the cold flakes. He bounded around the team repeating the action. Agent Dean called him to the spot Rick had cleared. He sniffed and immediately sat in the snow. He wagged his tail and barked.

"Good boy, Bax." Kendra looked up at Rick. "Agent Stone was here. He's telling us that, but I don't know if he will be able to tell us where he went from here."

Rick nodded, encouraged by the fact that Baxter caught Jack's scent at all. It gave them a place to start. He addressed his team. "Make your way down to the bottom of the ravine. See if you find anything. Be careful not to destroy the trail."

"I'll go down there too." Dean offered. "If, as you say, the trail ended at the edge of the gully, maybe he fell?"

Rick's head snapped up. "I didn't see any sign of him falling. No scuff marks, no torn away stones."

Shit. If Jack fell and was lying hurt so close to where Rick gave up, he'd never forgive himself. "Let's go!"

Kendra rigged Baxter to a special sling that allowed her to rappel with him down the cliff. Rick followed them down. The descent was slower than Rick liked but the rocks were slick with snow. Below, the team searched the floor of the ravine. The canopy of pines kept the snowfall to a minimum down in the gully. Only six to twelve inches covered the ground at the base of the cliff. Rick peered up, calculating where, if Jack fell, he would have landed. Once again, Kendra gave her dog the scent.

Nose to the ground, Baxter scampered about, stopping and starting again, but with a definite intention. The dog became more agitated, whining and circling. Finally, he sat down and barked.

"What is it, boy? Did you find something?" Kendra leaned down to her dog and ruffled his ears. "Good dog. Good boy, Bax." He barked.

Rick fell to his knees at the spot the dog indicated and brushed the snow aside. His whole body stilled and a sickening shudder coursed through him. "There's blood."

The unit interrupted their search and joined Rick at the find. "Baxter found blood. We have to assume this is Jack's, and it's good news his body isn't here. It means he survived the fall." Rick swallowed hard and wiped his face on his arm. What he didn't say was the blood meant he was hurt, and an injury cut his chances of surviving in these extreme conditions dramatically.

"We need to clear this area, but be careful not to disturb any evidence. Shovel the bulk of the snow, but use a brush when you get near the ground. If

Jack's bleeding, he left a trail. Also—it's Jack. He will have purposely left us a trail to find him, and he would have tried to find shelter. Look for anywhere he might have found it." Rick muttered a quick prayer under his breath before he started clearing more of the rocky area where Baxter found the blood stain.

"Amen." Kendra agreed from behind him.

Rick glanced at her and flashed a bashful smile. He usually kept his faith to himself.

Kendra assessed him as he rose to his feet. "You and Agent Stone are close?"

"Yeah. He's the best guy I know." Rick stared into her dark eyes. "We have to find him."

"Let's get at it then." Her smile reassured him. "Now that Bax has the scent of his blood, it should be easier for him to track. Blood gives off a strong odor." Kendra unclipped Baxter's lead from his collar and let him sniff around the search area.

Within the hour, brutal winds whipped the mountainside blowing the falling snow and swirling it with flakes already on the ground. The temperature dropped to -10F but the wind-chill was deadly, at around -36F. Rick wanted to stay out and continue searching, but he was responsible for each member of the search and rescue team. As it was, it would be difficult traveling back to the compound.

Kendra approached him and shouted to be heard over the wind. "I have to get Baxter back to basecamp. It is too cold for him, and he's exhausted. I know you don't want to quit, Sanchez, but we have to."

Rick ground his teeth, despising the taste of defeat. "You're right." He turned his face to the sky and yelled "Jack!" into the storm. The only answer was a frigid howling wind that stung his cheeks. "Jack!" He tried again and hung his head. "Damn it. I know you're right. Let's gather the team and head down."

"We'll find him." Kendra gripped his arm. "If he's found shelter, he's better off than we are right now. Your SAC told me he doesn't know a better survivalist than Agent Stone." She gave him a second squeeze. "Keep the faith, Rick."

"Thanks." Rick called to the squad, and they gathered at the snowmobiles. "Let's head in. Take it slow and easy. Visibility is practically nil." At this point, Rick worried about getting everyone off the mountain safely before the looming darkness made it impossible.

CHAPTER 6

Laurel took a deep breath of the refreshing air in the passageway on her way to check on her horse. She closed the cabin door tight behind her and leaned against it for a moment before she went into the barn. It was cozy in Wisaka's stall. The snowpack kept the cold wind from creeping through the cracks in the wood. Her horse kept warm in her blanket and Laurel tossed her several leaves of hay.

"Hello, girl. How're you getting on in here?" Laurel scratched her horse behind her ears and received a nicker in return. "What do *you* think of the bloke in the cabin?" Wisaka nudged her leg and went on munching her grass. "He judges me for staying here." Laurel sighed and slipped Wisaka's blanket off. She ran a curry comb across her horse's back and withers. "How can I make him understand that even if I *could* have run, I couldna' leave you or the children behind? God knows what might have happened to you lot." She patted her horse's shoulder and scooped some grain into her feed bin. "They have my da in custody now—I'm finally free. I suppose I should feel bad for him, but I just feel numb." With the manure fork, Laurel tidied the stall as best she could with no access to the out-of-doors. She replaced Wisaka's blanket for the night. Tomorrow, she'd have to start digging out.

"Well, here goes. Wish me luck. Have a good sleep, Saka." Laurel headed into the cabin. "See you in the morning."

Jack was still sitting on the bed when she returned.

"She okay?"

"Snug as a bug." Laurel pushed the kettle over the fire. "Cuppa?"

"Any coffee left?"

Laurel turned to check the pot on the stove. "I'll heat it."

"No chance you have any whiskey stashed away, is there?"

She smiled at that. "What kind of Scotswoman would I be without a wee dram or two." In fact, a little nip of scotch in her tea sounded like the perfect plan.

Once they had their hot drinks, Laurel settled into the overstuffed chair by the fire. She drew her knees up underneath herself and faced Jack.

"So, you wanna know how I came to be living in a compound filled with hate?" Laurel hoped to sound flippant, but Jack frowned and his eyes narrowed. She took a deep breath, gaining strength from the whisky tickling her nose in the rising steam. The warm, buttery dram of scotch in her tea relaxed her. "I'll start at the beginning. My mam met my father in Edinburgh one summer about twenty-six years ago.

They'd both come from the countryside to find work at the festivals in the city during August. Thousands of tourists flood in, so consequently there's more jobs for the locals." She took a fortifying sip of her hot toddy.

"My da got a job giving tours of old town and he met my mam at the pub where she worked. One thing led to another, they fancied themselves in love, and they married. Before long, I appeared on the scene, and with me, reality crashed in. Another mouth to feed. They had nothin' to their names, so my da went to America to seek his fortune."

"Did he find it?"

"No. For several years he sent money to my mam, but after a while the funds dwindled to an occasional empty letter." She shifted to keep her feet from falling asleep. "We didn't have much, but I don't remember feeling like I had to go without. We lived with my grand-da and that helped." Laurel stared into the fire for a while, collecting her thoughts and Jack remained silent. She appreciated him giving her time. The fire popped on a pocket of pine sap and brought Laurel back to the present.

"But, after he passed away, I became a somewhat rebellious teen. My mam must have complained to my da, because the next thing I knew, a man whom I'd never met arrived on our doorstep claiming to be my father. My mam told me they had agreed I should go to America for the summer with him and get to know him." She searched Jack's eyes. "I was terrified."

"Your mom sent you off with a stranger? To another country?"

Laurel's chest swelled with a desire to defend her mother. "Maybe *somewhat* rebellious is putting it mildly. I started going with a bad crowd and my mam said she wasn't having it. She wanted to save me from them. Anyway, Roger wasn't a stranger to her—just to me."

Jack breathed in and adjusted his position to get comfortable. "Go on."

"So, my mam produced a passport she'd ordered for me and the next day, I sat on a plane bound for America. Truth be told, I was scared, but excited too. It was meant to be a grand adventure. Or so I thought." Laurel drained her cup and stretched. "Long story short, we flew to Seattle and then drove for hours and hours, deep into the woods until we arrived at the compound. My father took my passport and mobile and kept me locked in his house. He told me it was for my own good. That I needed to learn some discipline and respect. Apparently, I didn't improve fast enough, and they sent me to the pit to learn my lesson." Laurel fell silent as dark memories of the abuse in those first months flooded her mind.

"What's the pit?" Jack waited for her to say more, but when she didn't answer he moved on. "How about your mom? What did she do?"

Laurel's throat stuck on a hard lump and tears stung her eyes. "I don't know." She cleared her throat. "I haven't talked to her since. It's been almost ten years." Her anguished gaze rushed to Jack's. "I don't know if she was keen to get rid of me or if she had no idea what happened to me. I've had no way to contact her until one day, over a month ago, I stole my da's mobile. First, I called the police, to tell them about the bombing. Then I searched his contacts for my mam's number. I dialed, and it rang three times before I heard my father coming and I had to put his mobile back."

Jack's face was impassive. She couldn't tell if he believed her. "That's quite a story," he said, his voice low and quiet.

Heat flushed her face. "Well, it's true, whether you believe me or not." She stood and took her cup to the kitchen keeping her back to Jack until the tears in her eyes dried and she got control of her emotions.

"What about your horse? How does she play into this story?"

Laurel turned and leaned against the sink board, shaking her head. "There's a lot more men than women on the compound. Obviously. All the other women are married with families. So, some interested men have offered my father gifts over the years, hoping for my hand." Laurel shuddered at the thought of marrying any of those hate-filled mongrels. "I refused all of them, but my da kept the gifts anyway. I don't think he wanted to marry me off. He liked having me take care of his house. Anyway, one of the gifts was Wisaka. The man who drove the car carrying the bomb offered her to my father.

"My da wanted nothing to do with a horse, but he allowed me to keep her. Then one day, about two years ago, he brought me up here. He said he felt, after the past eight years, he could finally trust me. After showing me the cabin, he told me nobody else knew anything about it, not even Jedediah. If anything bad ever happened, if the government ever invaded, we could bug-out to this cabin and be safe." Laurel approached the fireplace. "Gradually, after he knew I could protect myself with a shotgun, he started to allow me to come up here on my own. Lately, since Jed and my da have been preoccupied with the failed bombing, I've been able to sneak up here a lot."

Jack studied Laurel, and she felt the weight of his consideration as he pondered her story. Finally, he spoke, "That's a lot to swallow. There's a lot of holes."

"Like what?" It shouldn't matter to her if he believed her or not, but it did.

"Like, if you had a horse and the freedom to ride up here, why didn't you run away?" Jack grimaced at the exertion of his question and sucked air in through his teeth.

Laurel answered in a whisper. "I was afraid."

"How'd your dad get mixed up with Jedediah Hotchkiss in the first place?" Jack sipped his drink. He rested his head on the pillow and closed his eyelids, pain deepening the creases around them.

"I'm not exactly sure. I think they met at a gun show." Laurel leaned her forearms on the back of the soft chair. "Do you want more Tylenol?"

Jack let out a long breath. "Yeah, that might help."

"And a fresh snow pack?"

Jack opened his eyes a slit, and the firelight glinted off the sapphire blue fringed with his long, dark lashes. Laurel drew in a breath and turned away. She busied herself with the pills, buying time for her heart to stop skittering.

"That'd be great. If you don't mind."

Keeping her back to him she shrugged. "Of course not." She brought him the medicine and when his fingers touched her palm as he took them from her, kisses of fire leapt along her nerves and settled into a slow burn deep in her core. It was all she could do not to snatch her hand away, or worse, clasp onto his. Her gaze flew up to his to see if he noticed anything.

Jack's expression gave nothing away, but he looked deep into her eyes. She felt exposed and couldn't hold his gaze. She turned and rushed to get the oil cloth, almost running to the door with her pot to scoop more snow.

"Are you okay?" Jack's voice sounded deep and rich behind her.

She shuddered in a delicious, dangerous way. "Of course. Why do you ask?" Her heart scampered.

"You seem nervous all of a sudden."

"Why would I be nervous?" She turned around and forced a tight laugh out of her throat. "It's completely ordinary for me to be interrogated by the FBI. It's no big deal at all."

"Interrogated?" The side of his mouth rounded into a grin. "You voluntarily telling me your life story isn't anything close to being interrogated." Jack's eyes hardened and that wonderful smile disappeared. "I'm not sure you're telling me everything though."

"Like?"

"Well, it's hard to believe you've lived among a group of Nazis for ten years and haven't taken on their belief system, for one thing."

Laurel felt a rush of ice water pour through her body at what he implied. But seconds later, a reactive blaze of heat evaporated her abasement. "I will never see the world the way they do. I can't stomach the hate or the self-aggrandizement of those fools. How dare you suggest you know *anything* at all about me and what I believe in?" She tossed the snow pack at him.

He caught the bundle with one hand but it cost

him. He grunted against the pain. A shimmer of guilt flashed through her but she shook it away.

"I'm just saying it's hard to believe. These kinds of groups are similar to cults and they have powerful systems of brainwashing. How did you avoid that?" Jack rested his head against the snow pillow and eased his eyes to slits.

"No one ever tried to force me to believe anything. Of course, I heard the rhetoric, but it made me feel sad and sick. Mostly, I kept to myself. My father spends most of his time in the main building with the other leaders, drinking and scheming." Laurel's stomach turned to stone as she recalled her compound life, especially the horrifying first several months after Da brought her there. "Most of it was fear-mongering or posturing, until I overheard them plotting the bomb."

"And another thing. What kind of mother doesn't try to find her missing daughter?" His words came as a sharp crack across her face leaving her cheeks stinging.

"I—She—" Laurel's fingers flew to the silver charm at her neck and her mind clouded with all the excuses she told herself over the past ten years and a heavy weight settled in her chest. "I don't know." She slid down into the chair and whispered. "I ask myself the same question all the time."

Jack watched her from under his lashes. He moved the snow pack from his head to his ribs, but said nothing.

Laurel held Jack's icy stare until he gave in and closed his eyes. Her gaze glided over him. He looked like he could be in a movie. None of the men she knew looked like him or paid attention to details the way he did. In fact, she wondered if anyone had *ever* listened to her the way he did. It made her nervous, like she might say the wrong thing and sound foolish. Her thoughts rebelled. *Why do I care what he thinks?* But she *did* care. For some reason, she cared a great deal.

He drifted to sleep while she studied him. Laurel enjoyed the freedom of letting her gaze rest wherever she wanted for as long as she wanted. She watched his chest rise and fall, remembering the silky feel of the dark curls. Purple and blue circles radiated with smears of magenta bruising where the bullets hit his Kevlar vest. A strange giddiness bubbled inside her and Laurel realized she was grateful Jack wasn't killed and that she had him here with her in the cabin. She was even thankful to be snowed in. Yet, she couldn't reconcile with the fact that none of these things *should* make her happy or that she was ambivalent about her father's capture.

Agent Jack Stone was from the FBI. Wasn't he the enemy? They taught her not to trust anyone from the government. Logic told her she shouldn't believe the things her father tried to teach her, but what if he was right and Jack planned to take her to jail? What would happen when they dug out of here? Laurel took a firm mental grip on herself, she could not afford to have any kind of feelings for this man.

Jack shifted with a grunt. He was awake and watching her stare at his chest. Her eyes darted to his and away. Embarrassed at being caught, Laurel searched for something else for her gaze to land on.

"I think I might be able to sleep better if you help me wrap this bandage tighter around my ribs." Jack struggled to sit up.

"Right." Laurel couldn't meet his eyes. She moved

to help him re-wrap the bandage. Her fingers shook as he watched them touch the places she had been admiring a minute ago.

"You're trembling." His deep voice tickled her ear, and she shuddered.

He stood so close, he smelled fresh and musky, like the outdoors. It would be nothing to turn to him. To allow her fingers to glide over his cheekbones, his solid jaw. *Stop it. This is the wrong guy and the wrong time.* "I think I just got a chill. When we're done here, I'll add another log to the fire." Laurel rushed to finish bandaging him. "There you are. Do you need help to lie down?"

His eyes mined the depth of hers. She stilled, her breath hovered, waiting—willing him to touch her.

"No. I got it." He gritted his teeth at the pain, but eased himself down, flat on the bed. "You said MacNeil never told anyone else about this cabin and that Hotchkiss never came up into the wilderness, but is it possible he *does* know about this place?"

Disoriented, Laurel pressed her palm against her belly and took in a needed breath. "I suppose it's possible, but I really don't think so. My da said it was our secret—just in case."

"I'm trying to get a handle on your relationship with your dad. First, you paint him out to be a villain, a dead-beat dad who then stole you away from your mother, and locked you in a pit. A man who stood by while you were tortured in the name of discipline. Then you tell me he gave you a horse and allows you to come up to this remote cabin on your own." Jack spoke to her from his back with his eyes closed. "Those things don't line up."

"I can see why you say that, but remember, our

relationship has changed over time. I don't think he had a choice about my being sent to the pit, and he was the one who brought me things I needed in there. He used to frighten me. He can be awfully intimidating." Laurel sat down with a huge sigh. "But, I guess with time we've figured out how to be around each other. We've grown to care about each other, in our way."

"How exactly does he intimidate you? My partner described him as a scruffy little man. Has he ever personally abused you?"

Laurel cocked her head and drew her brows together. *Scruffy little man? Scruffy maybe, but nobody would ever call Roger MacNeil a little man.*

CHAPTER 7

A dull throb at the base of his skull woke Jack the following morning. Instinctively, he rolled away from the pain but his ribs screamed out at the movement. He gasped and eased himself back. Regulating his breath, Jack assessed his injuries. His head hurt, but not the searing pain of yesterday. His ribs were sore, and he guessed one of them was actually broken—the one behind the purplish-blue hematoma. His lungs were fine and breathing was only difficult if he moved too quickly. His legs and arms, though bruised in places, were in perfect working order.

"Good morning. How're you feeling?" The soft voice wrapped around him and he wanted to snuggle into it.

"Morning." Jack opened one eye. "What time is it?"

"I'm not sure. I don't keep a clock up here." Laurel tied her black hair into a messy ponytail and she wore an oversized flannel shirt. She stood in front of the stove, her long, bare legs catching his eye.

"What are you cooking?" His stomach stirred with the aroma of dark-roasted coffee and spicy sausage.

She glanced over her shoulder at him with a self-satisfied grin. "My specialty, bangers and mash. No eggs though. We're out."

"Bangers and mash?" He didn't really care what it was because he was hungry enough to eat anything and it smelled great.

"You know, sausages and smashed potatoes with gravy. Of course, they're not English sausages, but they're still pretty good." Steam from a pot on the stove swirled around her head. Jack was tempted to relax into this homey scenario where he lay in bed while a beautiful woman cooked him breakfast, but two things were paramount. First, she came from the enemy camp, and second, he had to go to the head.

Jack maneuvered himself up to a sitting position, noting that though he hurt like hell, it was easier to move. When he stood, Laurel turned and smiled at him encouragingly but then her gaze dropped and she spun to face the stove and stood frozen.

Shit. "Sorry, it just... morning," he mumbled. Laurel had told him she was twenty-six, but she'd been kept isolated from the world. She remained an innocent of sorts. "I'll just..." Jack made his way through the passage to the pit toilet on the far side of the barn.

When he returned, Laurel wouldn't meet his eye.

"Thanks for making breakfast," he said, hoping to engage her.

"Sure." Laurel smiled and seemed to relax a little.

"So what's on the agenda today?" Jack sat down

to a heaping plate of food and took a bite. "A man could get used to this kind of treatment." He winked at her. She surprised him with a pretty pink blush.

"I hope you enjoy it. As far as the day's plan? Well, after we check your injuries and change your bandages, I'll go out to the woodshed and get more wood."

"I noticed we're getting low. Where's the shed? I'll get it."

Laurel pursed her lips at him. "Right. There is no way *you* will be hauling wood. You're still in need of rest."

"I'm not gonna let you do all the work."

"You don't have a choice."

"But—"

Laurel held her hand up. "Don't argue with me. You're going back to bed as soon as you're done eating. If you want healing, you must rest."

Jack ground his teeth together. He hated like hell that he couldn't help. "My grandparents raised me to do my share of the chores. I'm not one for sitting around on my ass."

After breakfast, Laurel tended to Jack's wounds. Her hands were firm and competent, but gentle. "Your wound looks much better. I'd like to heat some water and wash your hair. It's still caked with dried blood." She rested a hand on his shoulder and Jack couldn't focus on anything else. "Okay, let's take a look at those ribs."

Jack stood so she could unwind the bandage more easily. "You're good at taking care of me. Are you a nurse?" He clasped his hands on his head, giving her room to reach around him as she worked.

"No, but I'm often the one folks come to when

they're hurt or sick. I've read all the first-aid and medical information books in Jedediah's library."

She bobbed in close to him every time her arms went behind his back to reach the roll. Her hair brushed softly against his chest giving off a clean, floral scent. When she removed the bandage, she peered at his bruised ribs, running her fingertips across his skin. His nerves sprang to attention in their trail. His whole system vibrated, hyperaware of her proximity.

"The bruising looks worse, but that usually means you're getting better. How do your ribs feel?" She propped her hand on his hip for balance as she studied him.

Jack's entire nervous system fixated on that hand. His blood rushed. He was certain this bewitching creature had no idea the effect she had on him. Jack turned away to look for his shirt before remembering Laurel had cut it off of him when she dragged him in here. A shudder ran through his torso at the thought of her removing his clothes.

Jack bit his lower lip and forced his mind to focus on the concrete tasks at hand. First, they needed more wood, then he'd figure out a way to travel through the snow back to the compound where the FBI would take Laurel into custody. Regret threatened to gag him, but he had to face reality. *Damn it all to hell.*

"Hold on. I need to re-bandage your ribs. Then I'll get you one of my da's shirts to wear."

Not wanting to constrain his tall frame in a smaller man's shirt, Jack said, "I can wear my jacket liner."

Laurel shook her head and smirked. "It's nae bother. Hold still." When she finished her ministrations and pinned the bandage into place, she moved to the chest of drawers and pulled out a huge flannel shirt. "Here, try this."

Jack held up the large plaid garment and knit his brow. With Laurel's help, he slid his arms into the sleeves. The shoulders and arms fit fine but the girth was for a man who clearly enjoyed his food. Jack tried to reconcile the shirt size with Rick's description of the man. "Your dad wears this?"

Laurel nodded. "See, it's a grand fit. Now, sit in the chair so I can wash up that dried blood."

Jack did as she asked and Laurel filled a bowl with warm water from the kettle. She gathered rags, soap, and a comb and brought them to the table.

"Can you lean back, do you think?"

Jack complied though it put painful pressure on his ribs. "Is this good enough?"

"Brilliant. I'm sure it hurts, so I'll hurry." Laurel draped a towel around his neck and poured warm sudsy water over Jack's hair. "You've got quite a lump back here. You probably needed a stitch."

"It's okay." Jack closed his eyes as warm suds sluiced over his head.

Laurel gently massaged his scalp without touching the cut.

"That feels good."

She dabbed the injury with a saturated rag. Her fingers were balm to the tight muscles in his neck that had yet to release from the shock of his fall.

Normally, Jack didn't like people to fuss over him. He preferred to fly under the radar and let others bask in attention. But he'd let her massage his head and shoulders all day if she wanted to. A smile tugged at his mouth.

"What's funny?" Laurel asked. "Am I giving you a tickle?"

Jack laughed. "No. I'm just enjoying this." He opened his eyes and looked up at her. "Do you do this for all your enemies?"

"Are we enemies, then?" An elegant black brow rose over her right eye.

Not knowing the truth, and not wanting to think about it, Jack closed his eyes and concentrated on her ministrations. Finally, she wrapped a towel around his head and declared him clean. He let out a groan of disappointment but let her help him sit up.

"When your hair is dry, you should have another snow pack on that bump." Laurel dumped the bloody water down the drain and put her supplies away. She added more wood to the fire and swung the kettle over the flames. "Fancy a cuppa?" She glanced at him.

"I'm not much of a tea drinker. Is it too early for scotch?" He winked at her.

She dropped her jaw in mock dismay and then couldn't help smiling. "Like I said, I don't keep a clock here, so who am I to say what time it is?"

"Great. I'll take a couple of fingers then." Jack went to the cupboard for a glass but Laurel shooed him away.

"Sit down. I'll bring it to you."

Jack did as he was told. He sipped the whiskey and let its heat relax the tension in his muscles.

"Would you like me to rub your shoulders a bit? I noticed how tight they are. I wouldn't be surprised if you have whiplash from your fall."

"Why are you being so nice?"

Laurel's brows came together and her eyes filled with compassion. "Has no one ever shown you a kindness without an ulterior motive, Jack?"

He held her gaze for a moment before he answered. "Let's just say it's not common. People usually want something. Maybe you think I'll go easy on you when we get out of here if you're nice to me now?"

Her eyes hardened at his words and Jack thought he might say things that irritated her more often just so he could see the flame ignite inside her bottle-green eyes.

"Quite right. That's it, to be sure." She turned on her heel, snatched her jacket from a peg, and disappeared into the passageway, slamming the door behind her.

Jack immediately felt a sense of loss. He'd been a complete ass to her after she'd been so caring. He ran a hand over his face and let the pressure of shame out on a long breath. She was only being kind. In fact, she had only ever been kind. "Laurel," he called after her. "I'm sorry. Come back."

She didn't return for over a half hour. When she came through the door, she brought a chill with her and without looking at him she went to the fire to drive it off.

"I *am* sorry," Jack said to her back. "I guess it's my nature to be suspicious."

"And to be a wanker?"

Jack laughed. "Yes, and to be a wanker, sometimes."

Her eyes flashed at him followed by an impish grin that stirred something deep inside his barricaded heart.

***

Rick and the search and rescue team were up at the crack of dawn. The blizzard had worn itself out overnight. Flurries of snowflakes still fell, but the brutal gusts and blinding snow had subsided.

Over a plate of scrambled eggs and hickory smoked ham, that he couldn't taste, Rick addressed the team. "We'll head up this morning as soon as everyone is packed. Plan for winter-weather camping. This time we'll be prepared to stay on location until we find Agent Stone. We're wasting too much time traveling up and back. I don't want to come down here again without him. Clear?"

Members of the team nodded and responded with grunts or one-word affirmatives.

"Okay, eat a hearty breakfast. Fuel up. It's going to be a long, cold day. Rendezvous at the snowmobiles out front by oh-eight-hundred." Rick scanned the mess hall for Kendra. "Agent Dean, do you have all the gear you need to camp with your dog?"

"Got it covered. We'll be ready by eight." When she smiled, a warm sense of confidence radiated from her and washed over Rick. He scrunched his brows together and gave her a double-take.

Kendra's smile grew, but she turned to leave the building. Rick watched her bend down to talk to Baxter when a dark-green dually roared into the compound. "What the hell?"

The truck pulled up in front of the main building, replacing the fresh morning air with diesel fumes. Two civilians got out and approached the steps. The taller man wearing a cowboy hat, took the steps in two bounds. His darker partner had a slight limp and took the steps one at a time. Rick sucked in a breath when he saw the second man's face. He could be Jack's twin if Jack were ten years older.

Rick met them at the doors right as the cowboy blasted through.

"We're looking for Rick Sanchez." The man's demanding eyes were the same color as Jack's. "You him?"

These men had to be the Stone brothers. No mistake. "Yes, sir. That's me." He stuck out his hand. "You must be Jack's brothers?"

"Trent Stone." The man shook his hand with a crushing grip then took off his hat and pointed toward his brother. "This is my brother Cade."

"How'd you get past the gate-guard?"

Trent grinned. "Cade flashed his military ID and we said you were expecting us. No problem."

Rick stood a little taller and moved to shake Cade's hand. "We spoke on the phone last night. I didn't expect to see you this morning." He glanced at Trent. "Didn't you just get married?"

"A honeymoon can wait, finding our little brother can't."

Cade stared at Rick. "Did you find him?"

"No sir, not yet. The weather forced us back to camp yesterday with white-out, blizzard conditions." Rick cleared his throat. "We're heading out as soon as we're packed up. We'll camp out there until we find him."

Cade narrowed his eyes. "We're coming with you."

Rick glanced at Trent and saw the same strong-as-steel resolve. He held up his hands. "I'm sorry, I can't take you up there. We can't allow civilians to get involved with the search. But I promise we'll keep you informed by radio, every step of the way."

"Like hell." Trent stepped toward him. "Last time I checked the FBI didn't own the mountains in Idaho. We're going. With or without you."

Rick slid his gaze to Cade who didn't say anything. He didn't need to.

"Listen guys. I know you want to do all you can to help find Jack. So do I. Jack's like a brother to me. I will find him. But you have to stay here at the camp."

"He may be *like* a brother to you, but he actually *is* a brother to us. We're going." Cade's low tone brooked no argument.

Rick perched his hands on his hips searching for words to convince them.

From behind him the SAC's voice boomed out. "You must be Jack Stone's brothers." The commander approached the men and shook their hands. "I am Special Agent in Command Jenkins. I want to reassure you we are doing everything we can to find Jack and bring him home safely."

"We're here to help." Cade crossed his arms in front of his chest.

The commander gave them a thin smile. "We cannot allow civilians to interfere in a search and rescue effort, gentlemen. I'm sure you understand."

"You have no authority over us or over where we decide to go." Trent's jaw muscles bunched into a knot.

"That's where you're wrong, sir. I'm afraid I have complete authority over where you go, or don't go, in this active crime scene and investigation. Now, please, make yourselves at home and wait for the professionals to do their job. We will keep you informed as to their progress." He turned to leave, but stopped at the door and looked back. "If you attempt to go against my orders, I will have you arrested." He closed the door behind him.

"Asshole," Trent muttered.

Rick looked Trent in the eye. "He's a good man, he's just following policy. I know you two could handle yourselves on the mountain, but I think you understand why the policy is in place. Most people would get in the way or get hurt themselves." Rick walked to the coffeepot and poured a cup. He held it up as an offer. Trent and Cade both nodded and moved toward him. "Jack told me he learned all he knows about tracking from you two. I know you live in this type of terrain. Because of that, you need to trust Jack. We're sure he's found shelter and is surviving until we can find him."

Cade's gray eyes leveled him. "You're sure, are you?"

Rick's shoulders slumped a little. "No. But I have to trust, and so do you. I won't come back unless I have Jack with me. One way or another." He poured a second cup. "Okay?"

Cade's voice dropped an octave. "You have one day."

CHAPTER 8

By late morning, Laurel had loaded a sled full of cut wood and pulled it to the cabin. It was slow going, getting the sled out to the woodshed, but once she forged a trail through the deep snow, coming back was easier. Jack insisted on helping stack the wood inside the cabin. Laurel didn't tell him she probably could have done the job faster by herself. He could only carry one or two pieces of wood at a time and she ended up waiting for him on several occasions. When he was forced to stop and catch his breath, Laurel could see his misery.

"Why don't you put the water on for tea while I finish up here?" Laurel nudged him toward the fire. He confirmed his pain when he did as she suggested without arguing.

Once she finished stacking the wood, Laurel put three fresh logs on the fire to reheat the room. Then she and Jack sat together in front of the flames and she sipped her hot drink. He closed his eyes and the muscles in his jaw bunched.

"You've overdone. Maybe you should lie down for a little while."

He nodded once and moved to get up.

Laurel helped him to stand and then to lie back down on the bed. His breath evened with sleep in the next minute and Laurel allowed herself to watch him for a time before she got back to work. She found a large bowl and took it to the front door. When she opened it, snow swirled in. The storm had started up again in a frenzy. Laurel pulled enough snow inside to fill the bathing tub and the sink and all the pots and bowls. She pushed as much snow away from the door as she could, but it was getting harder to win the battle against the blizzard.

While Jack slept, Laurel prepared the food for lunch and went next door to check on her horse. While the canned cock-a-leekie soup bubbled on the stove, Laurel took turns reading a novel and watching Jack sleep. She longed to run her fingers over the planes of his face, but she forced herself to stay seated in her chair. It would be embarrassing enough if he caught her staring at him again, let alone touching him.

He woke when she slammed the oven door shut with her knee. "Mm, what're you cooking? It smells great."

"Soup."

"Smells like bread."

"And buns." Laurel glanced over her shoulder in time to see him lick his lips and smile. She almost dropped the pan.

"How's the storm?"

"It's been snowing while you slept and last I checked, it didn't look like it planned to stop anytime soon." Laurel peered out the window over the sink but snow covered most of her view. She opened the front door. "There's a ton of snow out there, even for the high-country." The winds picked up and their bitter bite forced Laurel to close the door.

"I think, if we slow down on burning the wood, we'll have enough for several more days. Plenty of water. What about food?"

"I'm good on staples like flour, sugar, coffee and butter. We're getting low on meat, but I have plenty of potatoes, squashes, beans, and canned vegetables."

"So we won't starve." Jack rolled to his side and pushed himself to his feet. With a slight limp, he paced in front of the fireplace.

"Why don't you sit down."

Jack frowned at her. "I'm sick of sitting. I want to get out of here."

"If you try to make your way back to the compound in this storm, they'll find you frozen solid next spring. Now sit." He moved like a big cat at the zoo, all lithe muscle and impatience. Laurel admired him as she set the table. Are you getting hungry?"

"I could eat."

"Good. That will keep you occupied for a little while and then maybe we could play chess or put together a puzzle?" Perhaps if she found something for him to do he wouldn't be so cranky.

"This isn't a camping trip. We're not here for board games and s'mores. You're technically my prisoner." He tried stretching and obviously regretted the move. He sucked in a breath.

"You're going to go mad without something to occupy your mind, and besides, I think it's more accurate to say that you're *my* prisoner."

He spun toward her and glowered, but he couldn't hold the expression as laughter sparked in his eyes. The grin that spread across his lips caused Laurel's heart to stutter. "You play chess?"

"Don't sound so surprised. I'm pretty good."

"We'll see about that." He arched a dark brow. "Challenge accepted."

Laurel brought the food to the table and they enjoyed their simple meal in companionable silence. She savored the yeasty bread soaked with melted butter. Wind whistled through a crack at the edge of the front door. The storm raged while they sat tucked safely inside and ate their cozy soup.

After lunch, Laurel collected their empty dishes and took them into the kitchen. "I need to check on Wisaka and make sure the snow I put in her trough melted enough for her to get a good drink." She pulled a jacket on before opening the passageway door. "Be right back."

It was a lot colder in the passageway and barn. Her horse nickered when she came close. "I'm sorry you're stuck in here, girl." But Laurel had to admit to herself she was rather happy to be stuck in the cabin with Jack. True, Jack was an FBI agent, but he was nothing like the kind of man her father and Jedediah always told her about. He was kind and gentle. Even when he tried to be gruff or was impatient, Laurel couldn't picture him as a thoughtless, brutal enemy. She wrapped her arms around herself and smiled. There was something about him.

Humming, Laurel checked her horse's water and gave her a bundle of grass. "Be back at bed time." She ran her hand down Wisaka's silky neck. Wood beams groaned overhead and Laurel looked up. She shivered and hurried back into the main cabin, and to Jack.

***

Jack breathed a heavy sigh against his frustration. He hated being stuck inside. His team was probably searching for him in the storm and it made him sick to think someone might get hurt looking for him while he sat safe and warm in a dry cabin with a beautiful woman. A wave of heat followed by a cool flush washed through his body when he thought of Laurel. Jack shook his head. He needed something to do, some way to feel productive and stop thinking about Laurel's fair skin or her glass-green eyes. *She is a terrorist. Well, not really, but she is linked in with them. She's the enemy.*

He lifted two logs from the pile near the door and grunted at the sharp jab in his side. His head swam and he braced himself against the wall.

Laurel rushed back into the room. "What are you doing?" Her eyes grew wide and she ran to his side. She glanced at the logs he dropped on the floor. "Jack, you can't be lifting things anymore. You're only going to make yourself worse." She slid herself under his arm to help him walk. "You're a horrible patient."

Jack gritted his teeth and breathed in through his nose. "I'm going crazy just sitting around. You shouldn't have to do everything."

"I know you feel helpless, but you must stop messing about and rest. Come on." She walked him to the bed.

Jack didn't need help walking but he wasn't about to push her away. He liked the way she fit, tucked in under his arm. "Thanks," he said when she helped him sit.

"I'll get the chess board. At least we can keep your mind busy—and humble—when I put you in checkmate."

He looked forward to the challenge. Jack figured he'd toy with her for a long while before he defeated her king. It was a rare opponent who could beat him. Chess was his game.

Laurel picked up the logs from the floor and stacked them next to the fire, then she pulled the bedside table out and placed a handmade, inlaid wooden chessboard on top.

"The games are under the bed." Laurel shimmied her slender body under the bed up to her waist. Jack's brows rose and his body stirred as he watched her backside wriggle, but he was quick to look away when she scooched out, before he got caught ogling her perfectly-shaped ass.

"Here we are," she said, holding a velvet bag filled with what Jack assumed were the chess pieces. He reached up and brushed a cobweb from her hair. "Oh." Laurel touched her hair self-consciously. "Thanks."

Jack was once again rewarded with the lovely blush. He wondered what all he might do to chance seeing that flush again. "Black or white?"

"Black, of course." A mischievous smile lit up her face and for the first time, he noticed a few faint freckles dotted across the bridge of her nose and cheeks. He was utterly charmed.

"The good guys wear the white hats. It's a good omen to be white."

She laughed and his heart warmed. "Black best suits the plans I have for winning this game."

They each set up their pieces and Jack moved his queen's pawn forward two spaces.

"Ha! I could have predicted that move three hours ago."

"You're pretty cocky. Who taught you to play?"

"My grand-da, before he passed away." A shadow drifted across her countenance.

The wistfulness that clouded her eyes moved him. "I'm sorry. Were you close?"

She nodded and moved her queen's knight forward and to the right. "Yeah. When he died, things began falling apart for me. That's when I started hanging around the wrong crowd. I feel bad about it now, you know? He would have been so disappointed in me."

Jack reached out and took her hand and gave it a squeeze. "Grandpas are never disappointed in their granddaughters. I bet he would have understood. He would have helped you if he could."

A soft smile played on her lips. "Thanks. I suppose you're right. I wish you could have known him, he was a good man."

Jack moved his queen's knight out onto the board. "Of course I'm right. That's how grandpas are. The good ones anyway. The kind who teach their granddaughters how to play chess."

Two hours later they were still parrying across the board. Jack was surprised and delighted her game challenged him so thoroughly.

"I'm deeply sorry to do this, but…" Laurel's eyes glinted as she moved her queen into position and then laid down his king. "Checkmate."

He flashed his gaze up at her. "Congratulations." He struggled to find words. "It's been years since anyone has beat me. I'm impressed."

"I'm impressed too. You're a tough opponent." She reset her pieces. "That was fun and helped pass the time."

"You should know, I took it easy on you that time. Next time, I won't be so soft." Jack winked at her.

Her laugh bounced lightly off the ceiling beams. "Is that so?" Laurel set Jack's king back to rights and started on his other pieces.

He helped. "I demand a rematch. Ready to play again?"

"You must be a glutton for punishment." She stood and placed a hand on her belly. "I'm a little peckish, how 'bout you?"

"Always."

"How about chili and cornbread?"

"Sounds good." Jack pushed himself up. His muscles ached from the fall and from lack of exercise. "I'm going to see how much more snow we got. Maybe the storm is over."

"It's darker than pitch by now. So unless the sky is clear, you won't be able to see much of anything."

Jack shrugged and opened the front door to a solid wall of snow pack. "Check this out."

Laurel stood next to him and they gawked together at the mass of snow blocking their exit.

Frustrated, Jack slammed the door. A loud groan, followed by a crack sounded from the passage way.

Laurel's eyes grew large. "What was that?"

"I'm not sure, but it didn't sound good. I'll go check."

***

The search and rescue team started their day where they'd ended it the day before. The sun made a mighty effort to peek through the clouds and chase the winter storm away. Deep drifts of heavy snow left the woods looking like a Dr. Seuss illustration.

Rick spread his map across the engine casing of his snowmobile but his gaze strayed to Kendra. He regarded her as she got Baxter out of his kennel and prepared for his job. Rick released some of the tension in his shoulders, relieved to have them as part of his team.

Rick addressed the squad. "Today, our strategy is to find the missing trail. We know Jack was here. That is a fact. And now he's not. He didn't just disappear, so let's find him." He slapped the folded map into his hand.

"I've been looking at this area map to determine locations Jack may have tried to get to for shelter. Be on the look-out for caves, rock outcroppings, fallen trees, even a rock wall. We know he's injured, and it's likely he's weak or even unconscious, so call out, but don't rely on him answering. He could be close, but hidden. Keep your eyes peeled and stay alert."

Kendra guided Baxter to the spot where they found Jack's blood yesterday. "We'll start here, can I get someone to sweep the surrounding area. Maybe we can get a general direction of travel."

Rick assigned two agents to the task of clearing snow and then he crouched down next to the bloodstain.

"What are you looking for?" Kendra squatted next to him.

"I'm trying to put myself in Jack's mind. If I fell

and was injured, where would I go from here? What would I do?" He peered up the cliff to the top edge of the ravine. "That's quite a fall. If he hit his head he could be disoriented, which makes it harder for us to follow his thought process."

Baxter sniffed. He took a few steps out in several directions, but continued to circle back in. Finally, he sat down and barked at Kendra.

"What is it boy? What did you find?"

Baxter barked until the team searched the area where he smelled Jack.

"I've got something." An agent held up Jack's pack.

Rick narrowed his eyes at the bag. "It's empty?" Why would Jack empty out his pack and leave it here?

Another man called out, "There's more. A belt, a fully loaded magazine, and a watch."

Rick recognized the watch. Jack wore it every day. The sight of it without Jack hit him in the solar plexus. More concerning was the magazine. Jack would never leave ammunition behind. Someone had stripped him of these things. He scanned the area. "What's that?" He pointed to a lump of snow covering a gray shape.

An agent brushed the snow away and picked up the object. He looked at Rick in dismay. "It's a smashed sat-phone."

Rick stared at the destroyed object and a wave of stomach acid sloshed, making him nauseous and burning his throat with bitter bile.

"It's so strange that Baxter hasn't been able to pick up a scent outside this six-foot radius." Kendra knelt by her dog and stroked his head. "Good boy." She chewed her bottom lip. "It's as if someone lifted him out of here." She glanced up at Rick.

An icy finger of fear traced the length of his spine. "Jack was tracking Jedediah Hotchkiss. I think it is highly probable he's been captured."

"I agree that's a distinct possibility. It's the best explanation of how Jack could simply disappear without a trail. Did Hotchkiss have a vehicle?"

"He was on foot when he left the compound. Jack tracked him—again on foot. But that doesn't mean Hotchkiss didn't have some type of transportation stored up here somewhere." Rick turned to the team and raised his voice. "Start looking for evidence of a vehicle of some sort. Tire marks or—"

A fresh-faced agent shouted, "What about a hoof print? I think I may have found some type of hoof mark, could be a deer or elk though. It's only partial."

Kendra rushed to the young man's side with Baxter in tow. "Show me." She crouched low and when she looked up, she sought Rick. "It's a horse hoof alright. Too round and broad for anything else."

"Shit—one of the kids said a horse lived on the compound, but it was missing the day of the raid. Jack reported seeing a woman we haven't found either. It could be she and Hotchkiss took Jack somewhere on horseback, they could be anywhere by now." He cringed inwardly at the idea of calling Jack's brothers with this information. They wouldn't take the news lying down.

Kendra spoke to her dog and directed him to catch the new scent. After asking for a sit, she commanded "Apport." Baxter sprang to his feet and held his nose to the ground. He sniffed and whined. The dog ran about twelve feet with his nose dusting through the swept snow. He ran back and forth and then sat down at the furthest spot from his start and barked.

"Why is he only going that far? How could the horse's scent disappear?" Rick's throat constricted with frustration. "It's not like these people are professional spies. Agent Dean, try to get Baxter to find that trail. Stay with it until he does."

Kendra turned to Baxter. "Good boy, Bax." She turned to Rick. "At least we have a direction to head in. That's one good thing—a good start." She asked for more snow to be removed in that general direction.

They spent the rest of the afternoon gaining ten feet here, five feet there. Rick noticed that whoever had Jack made a good effort to cover their tracks. Their search changed from prints to brush marks.

"We found something." Several team members waved Rick over. "Look at this. Two trees have been snapped off here."

"So?"

"Well, if you look at the front edge of the breaks, there are saw marks. Some type of serrated edge cut here. On the back side of the break, it looks snapped off. Maybe Agent Stone was getting wood for a fire?"

Rick stared at the cut marks. "No, this wood is too green for firewood, but it's a great find. Why would someone cut down two young saplings like this?"

"Maybe to build a shelter?"

"Maybe. Look for more trees like this."

By dusk, the team had only accomplished two and a half miles of track. Rick finally ordered his team to call it a night and set up camp. He was prepared to stay out here as long as it took. He would not leave these mountains without Jack.

Rick wandered to Baxter's kennel. "Hey, Baxter. Good work today, boy."

Kendra joined them. "Would you like to pet him?"

"Yeah, but I thought you weren't supposed to pet working dogs."

"That's when they're working." Kendra opened the kennel door and Baxter stepped out with his tail wagging.

Rick let the dog sniff his hand and then stroked his head. Baxter gave his hand a big, juicy lick. "Good boy. You like that, don't you?" In answer Rick received another slurpy dog kiss across his jaw. He laughed and the strain of his day dwindled to a more manageable level.

Kendra patted her dog. "I think this may be just what you need." She met Rick's eyes. "Don't worry, Agent Sanchez. We'll find him."

As the campfire started to give off heat, Rick found a clear spot and pulled out his sat-phone to make the call he dreaded. First, he spoke with his commander, apprising him of the situation and asked him to lean hard on MacNeil for information on where Hotchkiss would take Jack. At the end of their conversation, Rick swallowed hard and asked to speak to Cade Stone.

***

Laurel took a deep breath when Jack stepped into the passageway. He seemed take up every ounce of space inside the cabin with his presence. She fought to act normal around him, but normal was the farthest thing from what she felt. Her senses reacted to every move he made, every expression. Laurel found herself doing idiotic things to get him to smile. Thankfully, she won the chess game. *At least he knows I'm not completely daft.*

What is it about him? Laurel looked for excuses to touch him and then marveled at the electric response her skin had to his. She knew she should stop this train of thinking right away. Jack embodied everything she'd been taught not to trust. Only, now that she had spent over twenty-four hours with the man, she didn't understand why she shouldn't trust him. He hadn't done anything to harm her.

Of course, they were snowed in. Things might be different if he could haul her in to jail. He probably would tie her up and gag her then. A delicious shiver coursed through her at the mental image of Jack tying her. *Okay—that is enough.* Irritated with herself, Laurel refocused on cooking the beans for chili and measuring the ingredients for the cornbread.

Jack pushed his way back into the room from the passageway. "The beams are groaning under the weight of the snow. We must have got a ton." His gait was slow and gimpy but he looked stronger. He even had a bit of color in his cheeks. "I fed Wisaka while I was in there, so you don't have to." He sniffed. "That chili sure is smelling good."

"Thanks. How much did you give her?" Laurel couldn't look directly at him without blushing at some of the thoughts wandering through her mind. "No grain, I hope."

"No. I just tossed her two leaves."

"Sounds like you know a little about horses?"

Jack grinned. "Yeah, I was raised on a cattle ranch in Montana."

"Really? You're a cowboy?" Laurel chuckled. "How on earth did you end up becomin' an FBI agent, then?"

Over dinner, Jack told her about how he and his older brother, Trent, hadn't gotten along as young men and when Trent took over running their grandfather's ranch, Jack had left home to go to school at West Point.

"Did you join the Army after that?" Laurel picked up Jack's bowl. "More?"

"Please. This cornbread is really good. It's sweet." His smile twined down her spine and warmed her from within. He continued, "Yeah, I spent four years active duty in Army Intel. It was an obvious move for me to apply to the FBI from there."

Laurel set his second helping on the table. "Do you miss your ranch?"

Jack shrugged and seemed to close down.

"Do you have other family besides Trent?"

The light re-ignited in his eyes and he smiled. "Yes. There's Gran—my grandma, Mary. She and my grandpa raised us boys after our parents were killed in a car accident."

"Oh—I'm so sorry. I didn't mean to—"

"No, it's okay. I was just a baby and don't remember them at all."

"That's awful."

"I wish I knew them, but my grandparents were really wonderful. We had a great childhood."

"You and Trent?"

"And our oldest brother, Cade." Jack lost himself

in a memory before shaking his head. "I followed those two wherever they went. We sure got into plenty of trouble." He laughed and to Laurel it was the most warm, rich sound on earth.

"When was the last time you saw your family?"

"Only a couple of weeks ago. Our ranch is just about a day's drive from here."

"Will you go back when…" *When what? When we get out of here and he takes me to jail?* "Never mind." Laurel snatched up the dishes and took them to the wash basin.

"Laurel? What's the matter?"

"Nothing."

Jack brought the pan of cornbread to the counter and stood far too close to her. He brushed her cheek with his fingertips and lifted her chin so she had to look at him. "What's wrong?"

"Why are we pretending to be friends? As soon as we can get out of here, you're going to arrest me and take me to jail."

His gaze remained steady on hers. Her heart pounded. She tried to look away, but Jack didn't release her chin.

"You will have to go in for questioning, that's true. But they'll take the fact that you informed them about the bomb into consideration.

"What if they don't believe me?"

"They have ways to prove if you're telling the truth or not. Listen." Jack moved his fingers from her chin to cup her jaw. "Nothing bad will happen to you. I promise."

Laurel's joints melted and she swayed into him, her eyes never leaving his. He looked into the depths of her soul. She lifted her hand to his face and reached her mouth up toward his lips.

Jack cleared his throat and stepped back. The warmth that had been swirling in his eyes stilled and cooled. "Uh, can I help wash the dishes?"

Bewildered, Laurel stepped back. In the first seconds of cold, raw, reality, Laurel was mortified. She covered her hot cheeks with her cool fingertips and turned away—barely in time before tears dripped from her eyes. "Sure. I'll—I need to go check on Saka."

Laurel rushed through the door to the passageway. Jack called to her, concern filling his voice. That was even worse. Now he probably thought she was a desperate tosser. She would never be able to face him again. What had gotten into her? Why had she been so forward? Laurel ran to Wisaka's stall. She rolled the door open and buried her face in her horse's warm neck. The roof creaked and a cold drop of water splashed on Laurel's neck.

CHAPTER 9

Jack cursed himself under his breath. He had no business getting involved with a suspected terrorist. He needed to keep his head and maintain professional perspective. Snugged up in the cozy cabin, it was easy for him to forget this woman's connections to the men who tried to blow up an elementary school. He scrubbed the pot in his hand well beyond clean.

In fact, it was still entirely possible Laurel was the one who shot him, then brought him here as a prisoner. He needed to remember that. Maybe when the snowstorm hit, she pretended to be a friend, waiting until her father or Hotchkiss got here and could take care of him. It was a smart way to keep him contained until help came.

Jack searched drawers to find a dish-drying cloth. When he couldn't find anything in the kitchen, he opened the top dresser drawer. Next to a stack of utilitarian underwear, Jack noticed a journal. He took it and sat in the chair by the fire, leaving the dishes to dry themselves.

The first page revealed the book belonged to Laurel and sketches rather than words filled the leaves. He turned the pages with care because the drawings were done in charcoal and smudged easily. His brows drew together as he studied the first illustration. A girl huddled in a corner, and the walls around her were black.

Page after page were dark sketches—black forms on an even blacker background. The images disturbed him. Always the girl. In one, her gaunt face stared at an empty bowl by her feet. Another depicted rats crawling on her prone form. Next, the girl crying a puddle of tears. Jack flipped through several pages of distorted angry looking faces that appeared to be yelling. Fists framed the top of one page and boots lined the bottom. *Are these of the pit she talked about?*

He turned that page to find a sketch of Wisaka— the subject change jarred him. This sketch was a line drawing of the horse on a white background. It was the first depiction that wasn't almost completely black. It wasn't hard to see the peace she found with her horse. Jack turned to the next page and drew in his breath.

The final sketch was of him. She must have done it while he slept. It depicted him sleeping. Jack had to admit it was a close likeness, but it unnerved him to see himself lying there unaware of someone studying him so close.

Laurel returned from the horse stall. She wouldn't look at him and he was fine with that.

"It's late," he mumbled. "I'm tired, and I'm gonna hit the hay."

With panic in her eyes, Laurel glanced toward the

bed.

Jack stood and set the sketch book on top of the dresser. He took a pillow from the bed. "If you can spare me a blanket, I'll be fine on the floor." He tossed the pillow next to the hearth. "I'll set up in front of the fire."

Laurel's eyes darted to the book and then to him. The charming pink blush returned to her cheeks, but Jack turned away, refusing to be moved. A big part of him wanted to pull her into his arms and reassure her. He wanted to bury his face in her hair. *Don't go there, Stone.* Jack ran his hand over his face.

Laurel shook her head, her black tresses gleaming in the firelight. With no mention of the sketchbook she said, "You can't sleep on the floor with broken ribs. Let me."

"Pretty sure they're not broken. I'm feeling much better already." He dragged a folded blanket off the foot of the bed. "I'll be fine."

"At least let me get my bedroll. It's what I sleep on the rare times my da comes up here."

They lay in the dark, with the fire's dying embers offering a soft orange glow. Jack rested on his back and watched black and coral shapes play across the ceiling.

"What was Hotchkiss's motive for blowing up kids in an elementary school?" His voice came out hard.

Laurel was silent for so long, Jack thought she must have fallen asleep. When she spoke, it was soft and Jack barely heard her. "It was meant to be a distraction for the police so another group could rob a bank without interference."

Heat exploded behind his eyes. "All those young

lives—wasted for a *distraction?* My God! How could you be a part of that?"

Laurel sat up and threw her covers back. "I was *not* a part of it." She glared at Jack. "I rang the police. What more could I do?"

"I don't know—leave maybe? Tell the FBI everything you know. You live with a bunch of sick bastards. It's hard to believe you don't buy into their demented world view." Jack shifted to relieve the ache in his ribs. "Tell me, Laurel. Why do you stay? You choose to live among jackals. How can I believe you're any different—any better than Hotchkiss or your father for that matter?" His glower clashed with hers across the room.

Laurel grabbed the closest object to her, which happened to be the wooden chess board, and threw it at him across the room. Jack deflected the heavy board with his forearm and the movement made him cry out.

"Shit!" His arm retracted into his side and he squeezed his eyes tight against the pain. His breath came in shallow pants.

"Jack!" Laurel sprang to his side her eyes wide. "I'm so sorry. Did I hurt you?" She stroked his arm with the softest of touches.

Through clenched teeth, Jack seethed. "I'm fine. Just go to bed."

Laurel sat back on her heels, her moist eyes shimmering. "I *am* sorry, Jack."

He looked away from her, casting his gaze to the coals. His heart swelled with the desire to comfort her, but he ignored it.

"It hurts me that you think I could ever agree with the hate or the plots to destroy lives. I don't, I never have. I wish you believed me."

"Okay—then tell me where Hotchkiss is. I know you know."

"I don't know, Jack. Why wouldn't I tell you, if I did?"

"Because he's your daddy's best friend and your cult leader. You're loyal to him—even if you disagree with his doctrine. Otherwise you would have moved away from the compound years ago."

In a tiny voice, Laurel spoke as she rose to her feet. "My father wouldn't let me leave and anyway, I had nowhere to go." She stood, turning her back to him.

"You could have gone to the police."

"Sure, and how do I get to them from here?" She shrugged on her coat and moved to the passageway door. "I have no idea where we are in relation to civilization. If I left, the men would have tracked me down in a matter of hours. They would throw me into the solitary pit where my father couldn't protect me— even if he wanted to. I'd be open to all types of brutal punishment." Laurel disappeared into the hall and slammed the door causing the rafters to squeal.

Jack's anger lost some heat. He hadn't considered that Laurel might have been a prisoner at the compound. She hadn't asked to go there and wasn't allowed to contact her mother. *If any of what she told me is true, that is.* He shut his eyes and thought of the haunting sketches.

Laurel stayed in the barn a long while and Jack couldn't sleep. She always retreated to her horse when she felt uncomfortable—clearly one to avoid conflict. That trait obviously played into her decisions, but sometimes a person had to stand up for what they believed.

The coals settled to embers, and the smoke burned Jack's nostrils. He drifted in and out of sleep. At some point, Laurel came back inside. Jack kept his eyes closed, but he remained completely aware of her. She stood at his feet and stared down at him for several minutes before she placed another big log on the fire for the night.

Laurel adjusted his blanket to cover him better and whispered, "I wish we met somewhere else, in another time. You'll never trust me no matter how I wish I could change things." She trailed a finger down his jaw before she stood and went to bed. Jack's heart constricted.

He sifted through the facts he knew and tried to reconcile them with what he wanted to be true until his brain gave up the fight and sleep overcame him.

***

CRACK!

"What was that?" Laurel screamed out in the dark of night. "Jack? Did you hear that?"

He startled awake from the noise. "I'm not sure. Sounded like it came from the passageway." Jack shifted to his side to push himself up.

"Wisaka!" Laurel sprang from the bed and ran to the door. Without taking the time to put on her coat or shoes, she went in a flash.

Before Jack got to his feet, a loud crash shook the cabin walls. He ran to the passageway and threw open the door. A wall of snow and broken beams tumbled toward him.

"Laurel!" He yelled and yanked on the closest

broken beam. "Laurel?"

There was no answer.

Jack pulled on his pants and coat, and lit a lantern. He found some gloves and a metal bowl to dig with. Gasping with the pain of exertion, he hauled mounds of snow and splintered timber into the cabin. Every few feet he called out her name. His ribs screamed and breathing took concentrated effort, but Jack kept digging and pulling.

The night sky winked in at him from above through snapped beams that looked like broken teeth. The storm had passed, but left a blanket of snow too heavy for the small cabin to bear. He prayed Laurel wasn't crushed under the collapsed ceiling.

"Laurel?" Jack climbed up the mound of snow and pushed what rubble he could outside. He heard Laurel's horse call out in panic. "I'm coming, Wisaka. Laurel?" Jack sat with his head above the roof for several seconds to catch his shallow breath. Maybe he could climb out and access the stall from the outside door. *Maybe, but that would have to wait.* Wisaka was frightened, but she was alive, she could still whinny. Where was Laurel?

Jack eased himself back down and shoveled more snow with weakening muscles. "Laurel?" His head spun. He wouldn't be able to continue digging at this pace for long. Mind over matter only worked for short bursts of time. His body would shut him down to protect itself. He tugged on a long piece of a beam.

"Jack?"

He stopped to listen. Did he hear her? "Laurel?" He worked faster, ignoring the slicing pain in his chest. "Laurel!"

"Jack—I'm okay. Can you hear me?"

He heard, and his body allowed for one more burst of exertion before it forced him to double over, vomiting from the intense pain. He had to stop.

"Jack? We're okay. I'm with Wisaka. We're trapped but not hurt."

He closed his eyes and faded for a time. How long, he didn't know. When he came to, he called out, but he couldn't get enough air to yell. A clump of snow landed on his face.

"Jack, can you hear me? I'm through."

"Laurel?" He opened his eyes and saw the night stars through the hole above him. More snow fell from a growing hole near the break in the roof.

"Yes! Jack! Help me dig through. It's freezing in here."

The thought of Laurel running through the passage barefoot, wearing only a night-shirt spurred him on. "I'm coming. Hang on." He forced himself up, catching his breath on every jab of pain in his ribs. He took the bowl and dragged more snow down, enlarging the hole Laurel started.

"Are you sure you're not hurt?" He peered through the opening into the dark barn.

"Yes, but I'm freezing." She continued digging with a large grain scoop.

"We need a hole big enough for you to squeeze through. We're almost there."

"What about Wisaka?" Laurel looked up at him, her green eyes wide.

"She'll be fine. It's you who needs to get warm."

"Let me give her a full bale of hay and fill her water-trough with snow, then we can dig more."

They each dug on their own sides of the opening until it they made it large enough. Laurel pushed herself up and into the hole, but she needed Jack to pull her through. He gritted his teeth and through blinding tears gathered her in his arms. He sat back against the snow wall gasping, holding his ribs.

***

"Let's get you to bed, you need to lie down right away." Laurel tapped his face softly and then with a sharper slap. Jack's eyes opened but were glassy. "Come on. I've got you."

Laurel hoisted him up to a sitting position and slid his arm over her shoulder. She lifted, and he used her for leverage, finally standing. Jack leaned on her with most of his weight and she forced her legs to bear him up. They stumbled toward the bed where he slumped down, whimpering. Her heart twisted.

Shivering, she pulled off his gloves but left his coat on. "Let's get these wet pants off." She tugged at the legs until they gave and then she tucked quilts around him. "I'll get the fire going. We'll be fine in a few minutes."

Jack kept his eyes closed, his face taut with agony. Laurel's hands stung, she needed to warm up fast. The embers were still hot, so she piled on fresh kindling and as soon as it caught she added larger logs. She held her hands to the flame and warmed them enough to leave the heat and put on dry clothes.

Laurel moved the broken beams from the floor in front of the door, and closed the cold night out. Not wanting to waste a blanket, she tossed the tablecloth on the melting snow, to sop up what she could.

"You need to warm yourself up." Jack's raspy voice came from the bed.

"I'm okay." Laurel sat on the edge of the bed and took Jack's hand. "You saved my life. I wouldn't have been able to dig myself out. I would have frozen to death."

"How's that coffee coming?" Jack tried to smile, but it came across as a grimace.

Without thinking, Laurel laid her hand on the side of his face. He turned into her touch, his lips brushing across her palm. Not caring what he thought this time, she leaned forward and kissed his lips. "Thank you. You put yourself through incredible pain to save me."

His eyes glowed warm in the firelight and he lifted a hand to cover hers on his cheek. She yearned to kiss him again, but they both needed that coffee. Laurel stood but Jack kept her hand in his. "We'll make it out of this."

She nodded and smiled past the lump forming in her throat.

"Out of all of it—together." He gave her fingers a squeeze and then let his hand fall back to the mattress.

As soon as it was ready, Laurel poured two cups of piping hot coffee and returned to the bedside. "Here you go. Let me help prop you up. How are the ribs?"

He tried to laugh, but the obvious pain resulted in a weak cough. "I take back what I said before. I'm pretty sure at least two of my ribs are busted."

"If they weren't before, I'm sure the heavy lifting and digging finished the job."

They sipped their coffee and watched as the flames warmed the room.

Laurel turned to Jack. "What if the barn roof

collapses?"

"How did it look when you were in there?"

"I couldn't tell in the dark. I felt drips of water, though."

Jack pushed himself higher on the pillows. "Let's hope it holds until we can dig out. I think we need to get out when the sun comes up. Just in case."

Laurel wished they could stay holed up in the cabin together for a long time, but she knew he was right. "I'm not sure we'll be able to travel very far in all of this snow."

"No, but we need a way to get out from under the roof if it starts to go."

"What about Wisaka?"

"We'll dig her out too. When I stuck my head out the hole in the roof, it looked to me like we're buried in a drift. But there are places the snow doesn't look more than a foot or two deep."

"You should rest. As it is, I don't think you'll be doing much digging." Laurel touched his shoulder and let her hand trail down his arm.

Jack reached for her cup and set it on the table next to the bed. "You too." He pulled her toward him until she lay next to him. He tucked her under his arm and her head rested on the unbruised side of his chest.

"Does this hurt?" She felt him smile.

"No, but don't poke my side."

"I won't, as long as you behave and go to sleep."

With a low rumbling chuckle, he murmured, "Misbehaving might be worth the pain."

Laurel propped herself on her elbow and kissed his jaw. She kissed him again before he turned his head toward her and met her lips with his. "I want to… I want you, Jack," she breathed into his mouth as they kissed.

His breath came heavy. "God, Laurel. I want you too." He drew away and settled her back in the crook of his arm. "But not like this."

"What do you mean?" She struggled to push away the sting of rejection and make her voice sound casual.

"Right now things are confusing and emotional. I don't want to take advantage of you. I don't want to do anything either of us might regret."

"I know my own mind."

Jack's lips brushed the top of her head. "I know you do. I just want to protect you, that's all. When all this is all over…"

Laurel held her breath, but within seconds, Jack's breathing evened and he fell asleep. She savored the feel of his strong, warm body next to hers, knowing it was only a matter of time before he would consider her his enemy once again. She sighed, sad they had lost their chance to be something different, something more.

CHAPTER 10

A sliver of sunlight peeked in at the top of the window, the cheery beam promising the storm was over. Jack lay still so as not to wake Laurel, who snuggled into him, one arm draped over his chest and her leg looped over his. He smiled to himself, knowing she'd be embarrassed when she woke in such an intimate position. Jack looked forward to another glimpse of her blush.

While he waited for her to wake, he strategized a plan to dig out and find their way back to civilization. They could ride the horse or at least use her to pull them on the sled Laurel used to haul the firewood. Laurel shifted and burrowed her face into his neck and he laughed. She sat, pushing herself up from his chest. The resulting pain was worth watching her face change from sleepy bewilderment to flustered pink underneath a curtain of tangled bedhead.

"Good morning, bright eyes." Jack grinned at her.

She dropped her gaze and turned her head to the side. "Good morning." She ineffectively smoothed her messy hair and glanced back at him. "Take that bloody smirk off your face." She slid from the bed and put several logs on top of the smoldering embers. "Breakfast?" Laurel moved to the kitchen, picking up the soggy table cloth on her way. She wrung it out and draped it over the back of a chair.

Before long, the scent of fresh coffee found his nostrils. He watched her light the stove and set the leftover cornbread inside to heat.

"Cornbread with syrup?" Laurel glanced at him over her shoulder.

His stomach growled in answer and she grinned.

"There's some beef jerky too and canned peaches."

"Sounds great." Jack gingerly pushed himself up. "I think if you help me wrap my ribs nice and tight again, I'll be able to help a lot more today."

Laurel raised her brows at him skeptically.

"We can't sit here waiting for the cabin to fall in on us. We have to do what we can while the sun is shining."

"I know." Her tone was less than enthusiastic.

Over breakfast, Jack shared his plan. He dabbed the crumbs of cornbread up with his fork. Laurel wiped a drip of honey from the side of his mouth and he turned to catch her finger in his mouth tasting the sweetness. Their eyes clashed together with electric yearning.

Laurel smiled but then drew away. She touched the silver charm on her neck and then stacked his empty plate on top of hers. She cleared her throat. "We're a little over twenty miles from the compound. Normally, we could make that trip in one day with good weather, but in this snow? No way."

"True. So today, we'll just dig out an emergency escape route through the front and then one for your horse behind the barn. Maybe the sun will help and melt some of the snow off." Jack stood and stretched the best he could, wincing as his ribs complained. "We'll be able to assess the situation better once we get outside."

"Where will we put the snow we dig away from the door? The tub's already full."

"I think I can climb up through the broken roof in the passageway and dig out from the roof down to the door."

"I should do the digging."

"We can take turns. First, let's get the fire blazing nice and hot. That might help melt snow off the roof. Just in case though, we should put all necessary survival items, food, and weapons under the table in case we have a cave in. That way we'll know where it is, and it will be protected."

Laurel worked tirelessly all day by his side. They moved hills of snow. Jack took far too many breaks, frustrated by his pain and sense of helplessness. Laurel was inexhaustible. She dug, stoked the fire, made snacks, and dug some more. Jack's consolation in resting was watching her move, strong and efficient. By the time the sun dipped below the tree line, they had fashioned a snowy courtyard in the drift that had sealed the cabin's front door.

Laurel climbed the wall and peered over the top. "You're right, Jack. There are huge drifts but we might be able to find a path through the sparser areas."

"Good to hear. For now, let's call it a day." He

waited for her to climb down and go inside before he followed and closed the door. "The fire feels good, and I'm beat." Jack set his boots by the fire to dry and eased himself down on the bed.

Laurel brought a plate of left-overs to share and she sat next to him. "Want a chess rematch after dinner?"

"Somebody broke the chessboard." He winked.

"That board isn't broken, you're just scared you'll lose again."

"I let you win."

"Keep telling yourself that." Laurel's laughter brightened the whole room and warmed a place deep in Jack's soul he had allowed to go cold.

"To tell you the truth, I'm fighting sleep. Raincheck?"

"I'll hold you to it."

He smiled, laid back and drifted instantly into a dream.

***

Jack's face relaxed as sleep claimed him. Laurel cleaned up the supper food and then slipped into the bed next to him. She lay facing him, not allowing herself to touch him, though his warmth still comforted her. How many more nights would she get to enjoy the pleasure of watching him sleep? One, maybe two, before Jack insisted on taking her back to reality and most likely jail. Would she ever see him again once they were back in the real world?

It was so unfair. Up until now, her life dealt her a hand she never would have chosen. She didn't ask to be held prisoner at a neo-Nazi compound somewhere in the western United States. Laurel shifted, self-pity made her uncomfortable. In truth, if her da hadn't forced her to stay there, she never would have met Jack. Yet, even that became a double-edged sword, because she *did* meet him and now she wanted nothing more than to pursue a relationship with him, but as soon as he could, Jack would take her to jail.

No self-respecting FBI agent would ever want anything to do with someone who'd been convicted of terrorism. She hadn't taken part in any of the hateful actions, but she worried *that* fact wouldn't matter. She was guilty by association regardless of the truth. That's how the world worked, no matter what Jack said.

***

Jack woke at some point in the dark night. The wind howled outside and he pulled Laurel a little closer to him. She murmured some unintelligible noise, and he smiled. A huge part of him wanted to stay here forever, in this tiny cabin together with the feisty woman snuggled next to him. That was a fantasy though. Even if they could manage to hide away here, Jack had to let his team know he was alive. But, once he did, he'd seal Laurel's fate.

In his heart, he believed her to be innocent of the hate crimes. He saw no evidence of bigotry in her, but there was no real opportunity to show such traits here in the cabin alone. Or at least they would be easy to hide. Still, he couldn't believe she bought into the evil dogma of the neo-Nazi crowd. But again, ten years is a long time to resist brainwashing. It would be almost impossible for anyone.

Jack pressed his head back into his pillow and sighed. He tried to picture some kind of future with this woman. He wanted to spend more time with her and get to know her but he'd have to wait until the investigation ended. She would probably spend at least some time in jail. And if they convicted her of terrorism, who knew? Could he wait? Would she want him to? How many FBI agents did he know that dated ex-cons? A huge zero—that's how many.

"Jack?" Laurel's drowsy voice blew across his chest hair.

"Hmm?"

"Can't sleep?"

"No. My mind's running."

"Want to talk about it?"

Jack swallowed, he didn't know how to approach the topic, but thought maybe the cover of darkness might help her share. "I saw your sketches." He felt her stiffen.

"Those are from a long time ago."

"Will you tell me about them?"

She shrugged but didn't answer.

He sensed her drawing away and pulled her back into his side. "Please? Are they of you or someone else?"

"They're nothing."

"They don't look like nothing. There's a ton of emotion on those pages."

Laurel burrowed into him and nodded. "It was an awful time."

"Tell me."

"All of that happened when I first got to the compound." Moments of miserable silence stretched between her words. "I had to be disciplined. I'd been too hard for my mam to handle. They sent me to the pit to learn my lesson."

"What is the pit?"

"A dark, cold place. No light. No people. No food. It's a bad place."

Jack swallowed. He had stumbled into something he wasn't sure he could help her deal with, but he pressed on. "Your father put you in there?"

"He didn't have a choice."

"How long were you there?"

Laurel shrugged. "Months maybe. I don't know, I lost track." She shivered, and the tremor tightened cords around Jack's heart.

"With no food? What about water? Or…"

"I got some food, just not much." She was quiet for another stretch. "I really don't want to think about it anymore, okay? In the end, my da brought me blankets and good food. Clean water, even warm water to wash with. The times when Da came were such a relief." She swallowed and paused for a time. "When Jedediah decided I'd learned to be grateful, he finally allowed me to come out."

A simmering rage rolled over him. "Were you beaten?"

Laurel nodded.

"Did they…" Jack swallowed the hot lump in his throat. "Were you…raped?"

She shook her head once and whispered, "No."

Jack's muscles tensed. He couldn't see Laurel's face and he wasn't certain if she told him the truth. He suspected she didn't.

"It's all over now. It was a long time ago." Her voice rang hollow.

"I understand why you were too frightened to run

away." For her sake, he moved on. "The drawing of Wisaka is beautiful. You have a real talent."

"Thanks."

"And the last one. That's of me?" His pulsed bumped up.

"I hope you don't mind. You looked so… peaceful."

Jack let out a puff of air to relieve some of the energy building in his system. "I don't mind, but it was a little startling to discover it. I didn't realize you'd drawn it."

They lay together, each lost in their own thoughts. Jack fought with warring emotions and had no idea how to process the information she'd shared. He wanted to kill whoever treated her in such a way. It was an obvious tactic to break her mind and her will. It made him physically sick that her father set himself up to be her hero—the one who saved her. So relieved to be free, Laurel somehow forgot he was the one who put her in the pit in the first place. *How could a father allow those things to happen to his daughter?*

Laurel curled into him. "What will happen when we go back?"

He couldn't answer.

"Between us, I mean?" she pressed.

After a long minute, he sighed again. "I don't know. All I know is I want you in my life, somehow."

***

His words warmed her deep inside. He wanted her. Laurel smoothed her hand up his chest, combing her fingers through the black curls, careful not to touch the bruises. Jack clasped her hand and brought it to his lips. He opened his eyes and the sky-blue of a sunny day shone down on her. She stretched up to meet his lips. Jack slid his hands on either side of her face and held her with reverence as he kissed her, first tenderly and then with growing hunger.

Laurel propped herself up on her elbow and gazed into his chiseled face. She traced his mouth with her fingertip. "Jack, let's have what we can tonight and deal with what tomorrow brings tomorrow." She wanted to love this man who had fallen so suddenly into her life and then saved it.

"I want to. God, Laurel." He closed his eyes and flexed his jaw. Then his eyes flashed open again and pierced her soul. "But I don't want to do anything to hurt you. Ever. After what you've been through. Taking this too far, only to leave you in police custody? There are so many things wrong with that, on so many levels." He slowly shook his head back and forth.

"It's only wrong if your intention is wrong. If you were actually trying to take advantage of me, using your position of power to intimidate or force me, it would be one thing. But, *I'm* asking *you*. I'm telling you I understand the complications and I want this, anyway. Let's have tonight."

Jack squeezed his eyes shut and bit down on his lip. His heart careened against her hand. As he fought against himself, she wondered fleetingly if the pounding of his heart hurt his injured ribs. She ran kisses along his jawline, the stubble long enough now to feel soft. She kissed his lip where he bit down until he groaned and pulled her onto the side of his chest that could hold her.

"Laurel, I want you like crazy but... Are you sure?

Beyond sure?" His gaze was sweetly earnest and Laurel reached for him in answer.

He responded with an almost ancient animalistic groan. Rolling them to his good side, he cradled her head on the pillow and possessed her mouth. His free hand roamed her curves finding what pleased him— what pleased her.

Tomorrow would have trouble of its own. Tonight would live in her heart for eternity.

CHAPTER 11

Both she and Jack were slow to rise in the morning, whether from lack of sleep or lack of wanting to face the reality of the day, Laurel didn't know. She snuggled into the crook of his arm and pulled the quilt up to her chin.

Eventually, she stretched up to kiss Jack's cheek. "Morning."

He opened his eyes, but it was obvious he hadn't been sleeping. "Morning." He glanced down at her.

Laurel pushed herself up and climbed over Jack, careful not to hurt him. "I'll make us a hearty breakfast. There's lots to do today." She couldn't bear it if he felt awkward this morning.

"Yep." Jack's voice sounded flat and Laurel understood neither one of them wanted to deal with the harsh truth the early sun shoved into their faces. Last night was pure magic, but she had shared a lot— probably too much. The last thing she could handle this morning was Jack's second guessing.

In fact, Laurel determined to face the issues

straight on and without dragging her heels. What would be the point of delaying the inevitable? She tore a brush through her snarled hair, tied it back into a ponytail, and then got to work on cooking.

Jack stirred, but she refused to look in his direction. No sense in making things more difficult than they already were.

"I'll put our survival items and everything we need to take on the table." He set his pack down. "After breakfast we can get Wisaka out and attach her to the sled. Then we'll go. We need to start as early as possible."

"Sure."

"We should start out walking and go as far as we can so we don't exhaust your horse."

"Mm-hm."

"Laurel…?"

"Don't—Jack. Don't say anything. There is nothing to say. No other options. I know that, so let's just get to it." While the coffee percolated on the stove and filled the room with its roasted aroma, Laurel packed her sketch pad, pencils, and a few other personal items in a second pack. She swallowed an ocean of tears she refused to let fall. Tears wouldn't help anything. "I'll bring all the beef jerky and any other easy-to-carry food."

Laurel pan-fried beans and hash browns for breakfast and served it along with the last of the corn bread. She sat down to eat and though she usually had a robust appetite, she couldn't swallow more than a few bites. It all turned to paste in her mouth.

"I know you don't feel like it, but you have to eat. You'll need the fuel." Jack reached for her hand but she plucked it away. He nodded and ate the rest of his meal with efficiency. After washing his plate, he got back to packing the items he thought they might need.

Laurel carried the rest of the dishes to the wash sink and brought the boiling kettle to pour hot water for cleaning. She leaned into the steam as she poured, covering any evidence of tears. The rafters groaned, and she glanced up at the ceiling.

"Laurel."

"What?" She didn't look at him.

"This is what I was worried about. You're hurting and—"

"And it doesn't matter." She turned to face him. "I don't regret last night, even if you do. I'm sorry for you too, because it was wonderful for me."

"Laurel," in two long strides he had her in his arms. "I don't regret anything, except that you seem sad this morning. I can't shake the things you told me about how you were treated. I want to take all of it away, but we can't hide away up here together forever. I thought maybe you…" He pulled her into his chest. "I don't know what will happen when we get back down the mountain, but I'll do everything I can for you."

They stood there in that limbo moment, neither wanting to move. Laurel finally drew back. "We'd better get a move on."

Jack stared at her for a time before he nodded. He packed the jerky in his bag then cleared his throat. "Do you think your horse will pull the sled without any problems?"

Laurel carried the kettle back to the fireplace. "She did fine when she hauled you here, so I imagine she'll be—"

An ear-splitting, wrenching groan drowned out her words. The overhead beams squealed.

CRACK!

BOOM!

Laurel whirled around as a frozen gush of wind blasted icy flakes into her face. She threw her arms over her head and leapt out of the way. Broken beams and loads of snow crashed in as the roof imploded on the exact spot where they'd been standing a moment before. Laurel released a strangled scream.

"Laurel!" Jack rushed to her and pulled her with him to the far side of the cabin. "Are you hurt?" His eyes scanned her before he stared at the gaping hole in the roof above the kitchen.

"No, I was out of the way, thank God."

"Yeah. Well, there is no staying here now. If we want to be out of here before the rest of the roof goes, we need to hurry."

Laurel put on her winter gear and gathered the food she could reach. Jack collected the firearms and ammunition. "Anything else you don't want to leave behind?"

"Nothing I can't live without except Wisaka." She lifted her pack. "Let's go."

"Do you have a shovel in the barn or something we can dig with? We might need to dig a shelter if we don't make it to the compound by nightfall."

Laurel knew survival would be unlikely if they had to sleep outside after the sun went down. It would be dicey even with a shelter. "Just the bowl and the grain scoop we used yesterday."

They left the cabin through the front door and climbed the snow bank they created the day before when they dug out a space to stand. Laurel dropped her pack onto the sled and set her rifle next to it. "I'll bring a couple of horse blankets. Your coat won't be enough to keep you warm when the temperature drops."

"Sounds good, thanks."

Laurel climbed over deep, cumbersome snow drifts to the outside barn door they'd dug free the day before. She tugged several times before the icy hinges loosened and opened. Inside, Wisaka whinnied to her.

"Hello, girl. We're getting you out of here today. Laurel threw a bale of hay out the door and up onto a drift. She pulled the blanket off Wisaka's back and folded it on top of the bale. "I'll bring you some grain too. You'll be working hard." Laurel found a gunnysack and filled it with oats for her horse. She reached for the grain scoop and the coil of rope, and was adding them to her pile of supplies when she heard it.

A rifle-shot rang out, echoing against the silent winter forest.

***

Jack had followed Laurel, but he paused to stretch, making room in his lungs for a full breath. Something buzzed the air by his neck and with it came a searing sting. Before he registered what caused it, he heard the gunshot and Laurel yelped half a second later. He dropped to the ground and snapped his eyes toward Laurel. She leaned against the open door staring at her leg. Blood seeped through her fingers as she held her hand against her thigh.

"Laurel—get down!" Jack sprang forward and dove to cover her, thinking about his ribs only after he was airborne. He braced himself for the impact and caught his weight with his arms on the ground so not to take the full brunt of the fall in his ribs. He knocked Laurel to the ground underneath him, his cheek scraping hers with his beard. Remaining low, he shuffled Laurel inside the barn and shut the door. Wisaka squealed and kicked the stall doors.

Gasping in shallow breaths, he held her away from himself to assess her injury. "Were you shot?"

"I think so, but barely. It stings, but I think it just nicked me." Laurel loosened her grip on her leg and peered at her blood-soaked jeans.

"Who the hell is shooting at us way up here in the middle of a snowstorm?" Jack answered his rhetorical question himself in the same breath. "Hotchkiss."

Jack opened his jacket and shirt then tore a strip of cloth from one of the bandage strips he had around his ribs. He tied it tight around the wound on Laurel's leg to slow the bleeding.

Laurel gritted her teeth against the pain and spoke through her clenched jaw. "He probably thinks I'm helping you."

Jack reflexively lifted his fingers to touch the spot on his neck where he felt the burn. The bullet barely missed blowing his head off. "Maybe, but either way, it's me he wants dead."

Another shot sounded, hitting the wall. Wisaka reared.

"Laurel, where's my second magazine? The spare I had on my belt?"

Laurel bit her lip. "I left it in the ravine where I found you."

Jack was incredulous. "Damn it. Why?"

Laurel lifted her chin and her mouth formed a firm line. "Because, I wasn't about to bring any extra ammo for your gun along with us. You could have tried to kill me."

Jack shook his head. "I guess I should be glad you brought my gun at all." He ran his weapon through a fast check and snapped the magazine into place. "Your rifle is out in the open on the sled along with the box of extra ammo."

"There's another rifle, but it was above the cupboards in the collapsed kitchen." Her eyes were a turbulent sea. "What are we going to do?"

***

As if in response to her question, two slugs battered the barn door. Laurel swallowed a scream. "We're trapped in here." Panic skittered up her throat and threatened to choke her.

"No, we're not. We have at least two possible exits. Stay calm." Jack stuffed his SIG into the back of his waistband. "But first, I have to find that second rifle."

"I can squeeze through the hole into the passageway and get it."

"I don't think so." His eyes narrowed.

"You still don't trust me?" Laurel stared at him. "But, I'm the one he shot."

"Not intentionally, that bullet was meant for me." Jack's eyes were blue ice. "I want to trust you, Laurel. But I can't afford to trust you completely. Not now your cult leader has shown up."

Laurel registered his cold words with an ache behind her sternum. The closeness she thought they shared evaporated. She swallowed a wave of defensiveness. "I would never betray you to him,

Jack. And he's not *my* leader. I told you, I don't believe the things he preaches."

"We don't have time to discuss it now. Actions speak louder than words. Help me dig this hole wide enough for me to fit through."

"You can't squeeze through that hole with your ribs."

"It'll hurt, but it's better than being dead." Jack took the scoop from her and started to dig.

A distant voice sang out, echoing through the trees. "Laurel? Laurel MacNeil, who are you shacked up with in there? What would your daddy say about you sneaking up here with a strange man?"

Jack stared at her in the following silence. Then he whispered, "Keep him talking."

Laurel nodded and hollered back to the man outside. "What are you doing up here in the midst of a blizzard, Uncle Jed?"

"Uncle?" Jack hissed. His head snapped around to face her, his eyes hard under his furrowed brow.

"No—we're not related. It's just what he likes everyone to call him," Laurel answered.

The raspy voice bounced off the trees in the forest. "I was at my cabin when the storm hit and now I'm out hunting. Imagine my surprise to find you up here in this cabin—with a man."

Nausea swirled in her gut. "Where's my da?"

Her question met with silence before a bullet smashed through a spot on the door where two boards met and penetrated the far wall.

"Why are you shooting at us?"

Hotchkiss let out a crazed sounding cackle.

"Stay down. He's toying with us." Jack glanced around. He dragged a barrel to the door and wedged it beneath the handle. Gesturing for her to follow him, Jack moved toward the escape route through the passageway.

"What about Wisaka? What if she catches a stray bullet?"

"Hotchkiss would have to shoot through the barn door and the wall of her stall. Chances are that won't happen." He climbed up the wall of snow and pulled himself through the opening at the top into the hallway, grunting with each tug. He turned back and peered at Laurel in the dim light.

She pushed herself up to her waist through the hole to his side. "What's your plan?"

He panted to catch his breath. "I'm going to get that rifle and then crawl out through the front door. You need to keep Hotchkiss talking, but stay inside the barn."

"Where will you go?" Laurel's heart sped up, and she clutched his jacket. "You're gonna get killed."

"Maybe. But if I do nothing, I'll definitely get killed." Jack reached to touch her cheek, looking deep into her eyes. He stretched up and kissed her mouth sweetly. "I'll get out. I want the chance to know if trusting you was a good bet." With that, he turned and made his way to the wrecked kitchen.

Laurel watched him from the relative safety of the passageway. He pulled at a downed beam and tossed aside broken cupboard doors until he found the rifle. He stuffed his pockets with extra bullets. With one glance back at her he nodded, then turned and crept out the front door. Laurel rolled her lips together, her fear so heavy she strained to draw a breath.

***

Jack climbed up the snowbank at the front of the cabin up to the eaves. He scooted across what remained of the roof, staying as flat as he could and then slid down the far side opposite from the shooter. After landing in a mound of snow, his ribs complained, but adrenaline kept their scream muffled. The need to survive out-shouted his pain. Jack scanned the woods for a path to higher ground where he could assess the situation.

Laurel did a good job of keeping Hotchkiss occupied and Jack escaped unseen. The militia leader called out to Laurel and then fired his rifle. Jack closed his eyes and tried to determine the direction of the sound. It was almost impossible with the echo effect. Almost.

Out of habit, before he started off, Jack checked the chamber on the rifle and then did the same with the magazine in his pistol. Maintaining a low profile, Jack crept into the cover of a thick wall of pine trees behind the cabin, their scent sharp in the cold morning air. Snow muffled all sound, but it left tracks. He didn't have time to cover his trail. He'd have to hope he wouldn't be followed. It was fairly certain Hotchkiss didn't know he was outside of the cabin. With any luck, Jack would keep it that way until the last minute.

Hotchkiss called out again. Jack prayed Laurel was smart enough to stay inside the barn passageway. She would be safest there until he could subdue Hotchkiss.

Finding a path from shallow spot to shallow spot, Jack made his way up and around. His goal was to flank his enemy. As he narrowed in, he realized

Hotchkiss was moving closer and closer to the cabin.

"Laurel, tell me, where did you meet your young man? I've never seen him round these parts before? How do you know you can trust him? You know a man will say just about anything to get what he wants." Hotchkiss fired another shot. "If he's the same man I shot three days ago, then he's a dirty Federalé. I thought I killed him good—tough son of a bitch. You best not believe anything he has to say. He's full of lies straight from the mouth of the corrupt government."

***

Laurel called through the collapsed roof. "Uncle Jed, why are you shooting at me?"

The old man crowed in response. "I'm mole hunting. I hear we have an infestation, so I'm doing my part to help."

"A mole problem in the winter? That's not right, Jed. Moles hibernate in the winter."

"That may be true, but they were sure active in September. Now's the time to kill them, when they're trapped under the snow." Jed called out before he fired two more blasts at the side of the building. Her blood thinned and trickled in cold drops down her spine. *He knew.*

Laurel closed her eyes and sent up a prayer for Jack's safety. She couldn't simply sit inside and wait out her fate. Laurel checked the bandage tied to her leg and then reached for her hat and gloves. She zipped her coat all the way up, and standing off to one side, she cracked the barn door a hair.

"Come on out of there, Laurel, and bring your

friend with you. I'm eager to meet him." Jedediah laughed and fired his rifle into the air.

Laurel squatted low on her good leg, with her injured leg jutting out straight. She peered through the crack by the door. Wisaka whinnied.

"Sh, quiet girl. You're okay." Laurel maneuvered her way back to the stall and tossed her horse some hay to keep her occupied, but Wisaka was not fooled. She pawed the dirt floor and released a guttural sound.

"You got that horse in there too?" Jedediah hooted. "You ever tasted horse meat? They eat horses in Germany, you know. Probably what makes them Aryans so strong. The ideal race." The old man cackled with amusement and Laurel squeezed her eyes closed. Her body shuddered.

Another rifle blast and Laurel's blood froze in her veins though her heart catapulted to her throat. It hadn't occurred to her that if they could dig out, so could Jedediah. In fact, she'd become so complacent, playing house with the handsome FBI agent, she forgot why he was there. She forgot Jed tried to kill him once already, and that he would keep trying until he succeeded.

And now that he figured out she was the whistleblower, he would kill her too.

"Laurel? Where are you?" Jedediah sang. "I can't hear you..." His voice sounded like he moved to the front of the cabin. He fired his rifle, but the shot didn't hit the wooden walls. *Oh God.* "Jack!" she screamed. He didn't answer.

Laurel ran back to the stall door and slid it open. "Hang on, Jack," she whispered. "Please, don't be dead."

Wisaka spun inside her stall. "Easy, Saka." Laurel slid her hand down her horse's neck. "You'll help us, won't you girl?" Laurel slipped a halter over Wisaka's head and led her toward the door and the opening she and Jack dug in the snow the day before. If Jed was in the front, she could sneak out the back way. If Jack was alive, she might be able to find him, and they could escape on horseback.

"Steady, girl." Laurel peered out of the barn. Studying her surroundings, she saw no one. However, someone saw her. A bullet lodged in the doorframe inches from her head and she jumped back. Wisaka reared up.

"Where do you think you're going, little girl? We have rules about running off without asking. Now you're going to have to be punished." Jedediah's voice echoed around her, but she couldn't tell what direction it came from.

Laurel changed her mind. Wisaka made a large target and it would be impossible to get her horse out without her being shot. Panicked thoughts bounced around her brain. Where was Jack? Was he hurt? Dead? It was possible he ran to save himself and left her to face the consequences. Laurel shook her head. *No, he wouldn't do that. Would he?* Either way, Laurel couldn't get out with Wisaka, so she put her horse back in the stall.

Jedediah's words sounded closer now. They stomped up the back of her neck. "Come out with your hands where I can see them. I won't shoot you, but you *are* coming with me. You have to be made to face your sins."

If she waited for Jedediah to come to her, Wisaka might get caught in the gunfire. On the other hand, if

Laurel went out to him, there was at least a slight chance she could escape, or that Jedediah wouldn't shoot her, and Wisaka would be safe. She might also buy Jack more time to get away. It was foolish to let herself hope there could ever be something between her and Jack. He was a special agent with the FBI, after all. Her heart splintered into icy shards. She insisted to herself that he was alive. At this point, she'd be happy to have helped him. Maybe when he remembered her, it would be fondly and not as a terrorist.

***

Rick's head snapped up at the echo of a rifle shot and a chill ran down his well-insulated spine. He turned to the agent next to him. "Did you hear that?"

The man nodded and then they heard the echo of another report. Baxter barked twice and then howled. Kendra was quick to quiet him.

"This can't be good. Everyone lock and load. We're moving out."

Kendra ran with Baxter, her breath puffing steam in the air. She caught up to Rick. "Sounds about ten to fifteen miles away."

"Agreed. We'll take the snowmobiles until the last two miles, then we'll continue on foot. We want to surprise that bastard."

Kendra rested a hand on his arm. "It could just be hunters."

"I'm not willing to take that chance. Plus, if that neo-Nazi bastard is shooting at Jack, it means Jack is alive to shoot at."

Kendra nodded with a grim smile. "Let's hope so."

She went to load Baxter in his sled.

CHAPTER 12

Jack heard the shot and instinctively dropped and took cover. He estimated the shot came from in front of the cabin but it was hard to tell with the sound bouncing off the peaks. Mounds of snow provided blinds to hide behind as he made his way along the line of trees. The pain in his chest fired hot synaptic complaints to his brain, but he compartmentalized it. He had to focus on the threat if they were going to survive.

Hotchkiss taunted Laurel and fired his rifle again. Laurel screamed Jack's name. The shrill panic in her voice pierced his heart. He grimaced, knowing she didn't realize that screaming gave away her location, and there was no way to let her know he was okay without revealing his. Jack needed to get to Hotchkiss before the man got to the barn.

***

Laurel waited for several minutes and called out

to their tormentor. There was no sound or sign of Jed, so she crept out of the barn. Pausing to listen for movement, she decided action was better than waiting in a corner to be killed. Laurel made her way, limping from tree to tree, toward the sled where she'd left her rifle. Something big and hard hit her from behind causing her to lose her breath and fall to her knees. Rough, scratchy fabric scraped over her eyes and scratched her cheeks. Tiny specks of light made their way inside the hood that felt like a grain sack and smelled of mold.

"Jack!" She screamed before a large, heavy hand covered her mouth. Strong arms yanked her off her feet. Laurel kicked and flailed with all her might. Her panicked screams were gagged by the burlap and the strength of her assailant. Whoever had a hold of her tossed her about like a tissue in the wind. Laurel's efforts to resist served only to exhaust her. Her body jerked at the reverberation of another rifle shot. Fear—a sharp, frozen, bitter thing expanded in her chest.

She wasn't able to tell what direction she was being dragged through the snow. She fought, clawing and kicking. The hand covering her mouth loosened enough for her to find purchase. She bit the flesh has hard as she could.

"Bitch!" Laurel was rewarded with a growl followed by a sharp pain behind her ear. The moment she realized her abductor struck her, everything went dark.

** *

A third shot rang out. Jack was certain this one

came from behind the cabin, but that confused him, since he thought Hotchkiss was out front.

Jack heard Laurel's muffled cries. He knew then Laurel hadn't stayed in the barn and that Hotchkiss had captured her. His mind sharpened to pin-point focus. But, if she was captured—if she was struggling, then when Hotchkiss fired the rifle it wasn't to kill Laurel. The shot was meant for him. Could Hotchkiss see him?

He leaned his head back into the snowbank he crouched next to. His increased pulse rate pounded through his bruised brain. Desperation threatened to cloud his judgement. Jack rubbed a handful of the ice crystals in his face to refocus his mind. It sounded like Laurel gave Hotchkiss a valiant fight, but then after she cried out, there was silence. He had to get to her.

His weapons were fully loaded but he had no extra. And the rifle was iffy at best. It hadn't been cleaned or fired in a long time and he didn't have time to sight it in. In a low crawl, Jack made his way between trees and mounds of snow to where Laurel's struggle began. Keeping low to the ground, Jack crept up to the location of their brawl.

Blood, stark and shocking splashed against the pristine purity of the snow. Ice filled his veins. He rushed to the crimson stain and studied the tracks in the snow. Laurel might have been wounded again, or the blood could be from her leg. It was possible the shot came from in front of him instead of behind. The concussion disoriented him.

Jack slowed his breathing and looked at the facts. There were signs of a struggle. He estimated there wasn't enough blood to indicate a life-threatening wound, and he closed his eyes in momentary relief.

Perhaps Laurel had been too much to handle so Hotchkiss had fired a warning shot. Was it possible that Hotchkiss had dragged Laurel all the way around to his flank? It was hard to believe the older man could move that fast through the snow, let alone dragging someone with him. Jack squeezed his eyes shut trying to clear his confusion.

He had to find Laurel. Jack acknowledged the possibility that this whole thing was a trap. His mind scanned the full spectrum of possibilities, and finally he decided. He owed Laurel his life, and he would make good on that debt, or die trying. Holding his ribcage with one arm and the rifle with the other, Jack followed the tracks east, through the snow. They trailed away from the cabin and Jack followed as fast as he could while maintaining cover.

Approximately fifteen feet from the blood and struggle marks, the track narrowed to one set of footprints. The large prints were likely male, and it was apparent, assuming they were Jed's, that he now carried Laurel. No other tracks led away from the area. The extra weight would slow him down. Jack glanced back to the cabin wondering again about the shot he thought he heard from behind him.

He glimpsed Jedediah Hotchkiss, and dashed for cover behind the nearest tree. The wiry man had wild gray hair shooting out in all directions from under a wool cap lined with rabbit fur. His beard was the same, long and untamed. The grizzled neo-Nazi leader stopped to listen. Suspicious eyes panned the surrounding woods mirrored by the muzzle of his gun.

Jack didn't move. The old man did not have Laurel. So where the hell was she? Jack shook his head hard to clear his mind. None of this made sense.

"You still in there, Laurel? Why aren't you answering me?" Hotchkiss moved ten steps closer to the cabin and waited. The spry man's eyes darted around and spun to look behind him. *Why doesn't Jedediah know where Laurel is? Did she escape him?*

Another shot went off, but not from the old man's rifle. Jack held his breath. Counting all the weapons he knew about, Jack had his SIG and the spare rifle. Laurel's rifle still sat in the sled with their gear, and Hotchkiss had a rifle. So, where had that last shot come from? With new razor-sharp awareness, Jack drew in a long, slow breath, forcibly keeping his heart rate down while he watched and waited.

Maybe Laurel has another gun she didn't tell me about. Jack scanned the area, cursing himself. She could have easily tracked *him*. Jack's trail was obvious, he had only been thinking about Hotchkiss and of finding Laurel. Had he allowed his feelings for her to give him a false sense of safety? *Where the hell is she?*

He shook off his emotions and looked at the facts, reminding himself again, if Laurel had wanted him dead she would have left him to die in the ravine. Or, she could have killed him in his sleep at any point in the last several days. *But, she's desperate now. She may think it's her or me.* The instinct to survive could change a person's perspective pretty damn quick.

CHAPTER 13

Laurel gradually became aware of a hard angle jabbing into her belly. She pushed against it and her eyes flew open. It was a shoulder. She was slung over someone's shoulder like a shawl and his bones thrust into her gut with each step he took. She pulled at the rough fabric covering her face and she remembered.

"Who are you? Let me go." Laurel tried to push away.

"Be still, girl."

The man didn't give her an answer, but she knew his voice, and dread clogged her throat.

"Da? What are you doing? Let me down." Laurel squirmed against her captor. Laurel's voice sounded small like a bird's song floating in the atmosphere.

"Do I need to knock you out again?" He growled.

"Where are you taking me?"

He gave her no answer. Instead, he sped up and rushed through the snow causing her head to bounce painfully against his back. Laurel struggled against the man's iron grip. Finally, he stopped and dropped her into the snow. She pulled off the scratchy hood.

A huge mountain of a man stood over her. "Laurel Mae MacNeil, you have betrayed your own!" he boomed, his voiced echoing from peak to peak. "You will face the consequences of your actions."

"What are you talking about?" Laurel knew it was best if she could keep him talking.

"Uncle Jed and I will take care of the lawman who's been bothering you." The man circled her small, crumpled frame. He carried a long rifle in his right hand. "Then we'll take care of you."

***

Hotchkiss ran to the front of the cabin and crawled up the snowdrift to the side of the front window. He peered in. "Laurel? Where are you, girl?"

Jack slipped behind a thicker pine trunk and watched the old man climb over the snow and enter the cabin. Hotchkiss must have realized the cabin was empty, so he scuttled back outside and headed toward the packed sled. Chuckling, he bent down to retrieve the good rifle. The blood in the snow must have caught his eye then because he moved to that spot next and fell to his knees.

"So that's how we're going to play this then," Hotchkiss muttered to himself. He pushed himself to his feet using Laurel's rifle for leverage and followed the tracks.

Jack let him get fifty feet ahead before he pursued. At the end of this trail, he knew he'd find Laurel, but who had her? With the state of the disturbed snow, Jack was certain Laurel hadn't gone willingly. He hurried behind Hotchkiss, though the cold air in his lungs increased the ache in his ribs.

The old man's endurance on the uphill climb surprised Jack. He tracked him for an hour, over two ridges and down into a valley to a shack by a stream. Jack didn't see any sign of Laurel, or anyone else. A rock outcropping provided him with the perfect bird's-eye view of the ramshackle hut below. Hotchkiss called out before he entered the shelter.

***

Laurel's father grabbed her by the collar of her coat and shoved her forward into a tiny cabin. It had four walls with a potbelly stove at the center. Two sleeping bags lay on the floor. Roger MacNeil tossed her onto one.

"You've ruined everything—all our plans. How could you? Where is your loyalty?" MacNeil kicked her injured leg. Laurel cried out and clutched at her leg as fresh blood seeped through her pants.

Laurel tried to stand. "I thought they'd arrested you?"

The man forced a laugh. "Where did you hear such a ridiculous thing? I've done nothing illegal. Why would I be arrested?"

Laurel's voice trembled as she put weight on her injured leg. "A man, an FBI agent, told me they breached the compound. That everyone had been arrested, and that they'd tracked you into the woods. He said his partner found you and took you into custody." She sounded uncertain, like she didn't believe her own words.

"Why would you ever believe anything a lying,

corrupt government man had to say? He was trying to manipulate you. As you can see, I'm not in anybody's custody."

Outside a grizzled voice called, "It's me comin' in, MacNeil."

Her father shook his head and glared at her in disgust. "After all I've done for you. After Jedediah let me bring you in and give you a home. We took care of you, gave you a family and a purpose."

"I never wanted any of that. I wanted to go home—to my mother." Laurel ground her teeth together refusing to allow him to see her pain.

"She couldn't deal with you. She didn't want you anymore."

Red-hot coals flared in Laurel's belly. "That is *not* true. When we left, she said she loved me and would miss me. She expected to have me returned home."

"You're wrong. She asked me to come and get you because she couldn't handle you anymore. I saved you and protected you. And how do you repay me?"

The door to the shack opened and Jed stood silhouetted against the bright snowy outdoors. He cackled. "That's right. You've been mighty foolish turning to strangers. Especially strangers from the government."

MacNeil gestured for Hotchkiss to stay quiet. "We're gonna take you home and get this whole mess figured out. You're frightened and confused, but I'm here now. All you need is a little firm discipline."

Laurel shuddered. She had experienced his idea of firm discipline before and had no doubt in her mind she wouldn't survive it again. With every ounce of her will to live, Laurel lurched toward Jedediah, barreling headlong into him. The old man lost his balance and fell. Laurel felt his fingers clutch her arm, but she shook free and ran out the open door.

She didn't make it more than four strides before her father caught her by her trailing hair and yanked her back into his arms. He turned her to face him and shook her so hard she bit her tongue and tasted blood. Jedediah scrambled out the door after them.

***

Jack watched helplessly as Laurel bolted out the door followed by a monster of a man who caught her and jerked her back. *Who the hell is that?* Jack stared at the unreliable rifle in his hands and bile foamed up his throat. He couldn't make the shot from this far away. He had to get closer without being seen. They didn't know he was there, and they were focused on their argument, so Jack half ran, half slid down the hill to a clump of shrubs.

The grizzly bear of a man shouted. "That's enough, Laurel. Clearly, I will to have to teach you a lesson. As your father, I have to. You've forced me into this. It's for your own good."

Jack narrowed his eyes, wishing he had his binoculars. *Father? When Sanchez apprehended MacNeil he described him as a small, wiry man. The giant attacking Laurel resembled nothing close to that description.* Jack sighted the rifle in on the man's chest the best he could. *Explains the flannel shirt.*

"If you truly care about what's good for me, why were you letting Uncle Jed try to shoot me?" Laurel's voice wavered. Jack controlled his breath and waited for a clear shot.

"I's trying to shoot that G-Man you were hiding

in that cabin with you. Where is he, anyway? Did I get him? Or did he sneak away and leave you here to face your daddy on your own?" Hotchkiss held his rifle straight up and fired into the sky. "You better run fast, lawman," he yelled. "We know these woods far better than you." The man's brittle laughter clamored up the mountainside chasing his threat.

Jack shifted the rifle's muzzle to the old man's head, wondering again when the weapon was last sighted in. His SIG didn't have the range to shoot the sick bastard from his current position, and he couldn't risk firing the untried rifle so close to Laurel.

"The agent left this morning," she cried. "He's long gone by now."

"Why was he there with you, Laurel?" Her father reached for his rifle on the ground and lifted the barrel, pointing it at her.

Jack's heart drummed in his head. His eyes riveted on MacNeil's chest. Laurel cocked her head and moved closer to her father until she stood, completely exposed before him. "I found him, unconscious in the woods, so I brought him to the cabin to try to save him. I didn't know who he was."

"He's the enemy."

"I didn't know." She sounded apologetic, like she was appealing to the man.

What was she saying? Jack's lungs ached like someone had knocked the breath out of him. *Had she been lying this whole time? No! She was only trying to save her life.* In that moment, he became completely sure of her.

Roger MacNeil raised his rifle to his shoulder and took aim at Laurel. "You brought them here, the FBI, didn't you, girl? You *know* him. You betrayed us all and then slept with the enemy!" He yelled, his voice defying the muffling snow.

Laurel raised her arm as if to block herself from the shot. "No!"

Jack realized he didn't care about Laurel's history—or her motive for bringing him to her cabin. He knew her to be gentle and caring. The woman he spent the past days with was bright, funny, and beautiful. He wanted to know her more, though the little he knew didn't coincide with a hate-filled heart or even a brainwashed mind. He determined to learn more about who she was and he wouldn't settle for less.

Jack sprinted in an arc through the trees to a position about twenty yards behind MacNeil. He set the rifle against a tree and pulled out his handgun. Holding it with both hands he aimed it at the back of MacNeil's head.

"Laurel," Jack yelled. "Get down." MacNeil's' spine stiffened and his attention temporarily swerved away from murdering his own daughter. "MacNeil, your fight is with me. Leave her out of this."

The deadly muzzle remained aimed, unwavering, at Laurel. MacNeil stood still. "If that's so, then come on out and face your fate."

Jack took slow steady steps toward him. "I have my gun aimed square at the back of your head, MacNeil. Both you and Hotchkiss, drop your rifles. Now."

The distinct slide and click of a bolt-action rifle sounded and a crazed cackle followed the snap. Hotchkiss stepped out from the side of the shack. "And my rifle is aimed right at your heart, lawman." Hotchkiss moved into Jack's peripheral. "So I think it's you who'd best lower your weapon, boy. Or I'll shoot you to smithereens."

Jack's stomach re-coiled into his gut.

Laurel's soft voice pleaded. "Jack, put down your gun. Please don't shoot my da. He won't kill me."

Jack disagreed. He had seen the murderous look in MacNeil's eye as he leveled his rifle at his daughter. His experience taught him that MacNeil would fire his shotgun at Laurel as soon as he had the chance.

His pulse raged and Jack winced at the sharp pain stabbing his sides and head. If he didn't take these crazed Nazi's down, he and Laurel would never get out of this alive. If Jack shot Laurel's father, Hotchkiss would kill him, but at least Laurel would get away. If Jack fired at Hotchkiss, MacNeil would shoot Laurel before Jack could shoot him. He might survive, but no one else would. Laurel wouldn't. *Shit!*

"MacNeil, put down the rifle or I will shoot," Jack commanded.

A breath later, a gunshot echoed between the rock faces of the mountains before being shrouded in silence by the surrounding drifts of snow.

CHAPTER 14

Laurel screamed, and the sound pierced Jack's heart.

He had taken a calculated risk. Jack ran forward, shooting Hotchkiss a split second before barreling into MacNeil and knocking the man off balance.

"Jack!" Laurel screamed.

"I'm not hit," he shouted as he rolled to a knee and aimed his gun at Laurel's father.

In that moment, MacNeil bolted forward and grabbed Laurel in a choke hold. He tossed his rifle down and pulled a handgun from the pocket of his coat. He pressed the muzzle into her temple. MacNeil's eyes darted about wildly trying to see who was shot.

"Drop your weapon or I'll shoot her where she stands." Laurel's father tossed her about like a loose bag of grain.

"Da!" she cried. "What are you doing? Let go of me."

"Shut up, you stupid little bitch. You've ruined everything."

Jack blinked. Hotchkiss was down, but he still needed to gain control of the spiraling situation. He stood and kept his aim steady on Laurel's father. "MacNeil. Let her go. This is between you and me. Laurel has nothing to do with it." He could attempt the shot, but Laurel might never recover from her father's head being blown off right next to her face.

"Like hell. She's the reason you're here."

"No, Eugene Werner is the reason I'm here. He's your mole."

"Bullshit."

Hotchkiss moaned and writhed on the ground. "Roger, you gotta help me."

MacNeil hesitated and glanced at his friend. "Where're you shot, Jed?"

"My shoulder... my chest. Aaahhh!" The old man gripped his wound.

MacNeil fired his gun into the air, blindly releasing his frustration. Then he dragged Laurel with him to get to Hotchkiss. Crouching behind her and using her as a shield, he pulled Laurel down to the ground next to the old man. "Help him!"

Laurel got to her knees. Her hair sticking to the tears on her cheeks. She crawled to the old man, pulled back his coat, and gasped.

Jack clenched his jaw and swallowed. If only he could have kept her from the horror of what she saw. He knew from his time in the war that gruesome images of blood and shattered bone stayed with you forever. But now was not the time to think about that. In the confusion of blood and injury, Jack marched straight toward MacNeil. The huge man heard him coming and turned toward the motion.

Jack aimed his SIG at the man's head, and he slowed to a walk. "Put down the gun, MacNeil. You're finished here."

Laurel closed Hotchkiss's coat over the gore and stood. She faced Jack and held out her hands. "Don't shoot him, Jack. Please. After everything, he's still my da." She sounded like a little girl and Jack's heart cracked open.

"I don't want to shoot him, Laurel, but I will if he doesn't put down his gun."

"Da? Please," Laurel cried.

MacNeil started to lower his pistol, then in a flash he pointed it right at Jack's head.

The shot echoed through the mountains. The only other sound was the flapping wings of geese frightened into flight by the report. No one moved.

The eerie silence was replaced with a high-pitched keening that rose from Laurel's throat She dropped to her knees. "No... no... no!"

***

Jack sprinted to Laurel and knocked her to her knees, dropping in front of her. He shielded her with his own body, before leveling his gun into the trees. *Where the hell did that shot come from?*

"Stand down, Agent Stone. Do not fire." A deep, familiar voice called to him from the trees.

Jack recognized Rick's voice, but couldn't see him. Relief rained down through his limbs. Jack lowered his weapon. "Where are you?"

Like a Bev Doolittle painting coming to life, what at first appeared to be drifts of snow, moved into action. Men in white, winter-weather gear, appeared from behind trees carrying white and gray-camo'd carbines. They made their way down the mountain-side toward the dilapidated cabin and Jack.

Laurel rose to her feet and stumbled to her father's side. She cried over him as she searched his body for the bullet wound. Blood drenched the pristine snow underneath him. They had shot him in the chest and he was already dead. Jack knelt next to her and pulled her into his arms.

She placed her hands on either side of Jack's face. "He was going to shoot you. I thought he did. But—"

"I'm okay." He kissed her forehead. "I'm so sorry, Laurel. I wanted to take him alive—for your sake."

Laurel pressed her face into Jack's chest and sobbed while he held her, stroked her hair, and murmured comforting sounds.

Rick dropped to his knees beside Jack. "You all right, man?"

"Thanks to you. How long have you guys been out here?"

"We're camped about fifteen miles from here. We've been out searching for you. We came as fast as we could when we heard the first rifle shot." Rick clapped Jack's shoulder. "God, it's good to see you. I thought you were dead, man."

"You saved my life—our lives."

Sanchez raised a shoulder. "Don't worry about it. I'm sure it won't be the last time I have to save your ass." He tried for levity, but it fell flat in light of Laurel's grief. Rick pointed his chin. "That Hotchkiss?"

"No, that's Roger MacNeil. I don't know who

you took into custody, but it wasn't MacNeil."

Sanchez frowned and shook his head. "Bastard. Well, I suppose we have plenty of time to get to the bottom of all that now that we've found you."

Jack gestured toward the other man lying in the snow. "That old guy over there is Hotchkiss."

One of the two agents checking Hotchkiss shouted, "This man's alive. Medic!"

The rescue team worked to stabilize Jedediah Hotchkiss while Jack comforted Laurel. Rick smirked at him, leaning into his ear he chuckled. "Seems you can find women anywhere, man. Even in a snowdrift."

Shrugging Rick off, Jack leaned away from Laurel enough to look her in the eye. "I'm sorry you had to see all of this." He ran his thumb over her damp cheek. "Everything will be okay. We're safe now and these men will get us back to shelter right away."

Laurel nodded. "I'll be all right. It's not like we were close, but still… he was my da." But the look she gave him was one of bewildered confusion. Fresh tears streamed down her cheeks, and she swiped at them with her gloved hand. "What about Wisaka? What will happen to her?"

"I'll go back to the cabin and check on her. She's probably still freaked out by all the gunfire."

"I want to see her."

"You need to have your leg looked at."

"I'm fine, it's just a graze. I want to make sure Wisaka is all right."

Jack sighed. Laurel wasn't going to leave the mountain without seeing her horse, so he helped her to her feet. Though his ribs throbbed, he held her tight to his side as they approached the rescue team.

"We need a ride back to Laurel's cabin. She has a horse we need to figure out how to get down the mountain."

Rick shook his head and chuckled as he instructed two of his men to ski back to the snowmobiles. "Ma'am, you need to have a medic look at your leg before you go anywhere."

Jack squeezed her shoulders. "Sorry, you two. Laurel, this is my partner, Rick Sanchez. Rick—Laurel MacNeil."

"MacNeil?" Rick clasped her hand, but gave Jack a sideways glance.

"It's a long story."

When they got to the collapsed cabin, they drove to the back side of the barn and heard Wisaka pacing and stomping in her stall. She whinnied when Laurel called to her.

"We're coming, girl. You're okay." Laurel forced the door open and was inundated with the pungent odor of horse sweat. She limped toward her mare. Wisaka reared up when Laurel slid her stall door open.

"Laurel, wait!" Jack gripped her arm. "She's too upset—look at her eyes. Don't go in there yet, you could get hurt."

Laurel jerked her arm away from Jack. "She'd never hurt me."

"Not on purpose, but she's frightened. Let's give her a minute to calm down and see that she's safe."

Laurel shrugged. "You're the expert."

"Not really, I just don't want you to get hurt."

Rick arrived and entered the barn. "We have Hotchkiss and MacNeil secured to toboggans. Skiers have already taken off with them, heading back to the rendezvous point. We have more snow mobiles at the camp that can get you both back to the compound quickly."

"Good work."

"I saw you wince when you got up, Stone. Are you injured?"

"Not really. I'll be fine."

Laurel stepped into the light streaming in through the door. "He's not fine. He was shot three times. Fortunately, his bullet-proof vest blocked all three bullets, but he has cracked and maybe broken ribs. He also fell about twenty-feet down the side of a ravine and knocked the back of his head pretty good. I'm certain he has a concussion."

Sanchez narrowed his dark eyes at Jack. "It doesn't do anyone any good to lie to me about your injuries, man. You know that."

Jack shrugged. "I have other things to worry about and I'm healing fine." He canted his head toward the stall. "We need to take this horse back with us. That precludes a snowmobile."

Rick held a hand up in protest, but Jack cut him off. "We can't just leave her up here. She'd starve. We're bringing her down." His tone left no room for argument.

"We'll arrange for a handler to retrieve the horse. You're injured and need medical care, and I have to take Ms. MacNeil into custody." Rick stared Jack in the eye. "I'm sorry man, but you know that's how it has to go."

"No!" Laurel gripped Jack's sleeve. "I can't leave her here, Jack. Please. I'll come willingly, but let me bring my horse." Her pleading eyes shifted between him and Rick and back again.

Her urgency squeezed Jack's heart. "I'll personally make sure she gets home safely, Laurel, but Sanchez is right. You have to go with them. I can't do anything about that."

Laurel cast her gaze to the ground and Jack watched the muscles in her jaw ball up. She lifted her chin but did not meet Jack's eye. Instead, she limped past him, brushing against his bruised ribs. She walked out to the other agents without a backward glance.

Rick studied Jack as he fought to keep his face impassive. "Sorry, man."

Jack turned away from his friend, not wanting him to see his emotions. When had he started to care so much for Laurel MacNeil? He knew all along they'd have to arrest her. So did she. Why were they both acting as though there might have been some other outcome?

Rick dropped his tone. "I got you, man. We'll take good care of her, I promise."

"Yeah, thanks, Sanchez. I'll be right behind you with the horse. We shouldn't have to separate until we get to the snowmobiles."

***

Laurel had accidentally bumped into Jack's side when she pushed by him and she was sorry if it hurt him. That wasn't her intention, but she couldn't look at him. She'd break down if she did. It wasn't Jack's fault they were taking her to jail. It would have happened whether or not she ever met him.

This was all her father's fault. She was furious at

him, but the emotion did her no good. He was dead. In her heart she was thankful it was Roger and not Jack who was killed, and that admission came with crushing guilt. Her muscles shivered as though to rid herself of the sickening twist in her heart. Uncertainty over what would happen to her and Wisaka swirled in her gut, making her queasy. But, her greatest fear was she might never see Jack again.

She might see him in court, if he had to testify, but she couldn't bear to hope she'd see him in any other circumstance. What kind of lawman would ever have anything to do with a woman who associated with terrorists?

Jack's partner touched her arm. "Ms. MacNeil?" He draped a warm coat over her that was as light as air. "Put this on. It'll keep you warm on our way back to the camp."

Laurel nodded, but couldn't force any words across her tongue.

"You okay to ride on the back of my snowmobile for a couple of miles?"

She nodded and glanced back at the ruined cabin. Jack led her horse out of the barn. He had all new snow-gear on and blended into the background. He looked like all the other agents swarming the hillside. "I don't think Jack should hike all the way back. His injuries are far worse than he's letting on."

Rick turned to study his partner. "Thanks for telling me. I'll see if anyone else has any experience with horses."

"Saka's a good girl, she won't be any trouble."

Jack looked up in that moment and his eyes sought hers over the expanse of snow. He held her gaze and everything else melted away. Bringing

Wisaka with him he strode across the snow until he stood before her, never breaking their connection.

"I'm not going anywhere, Laurel. I'll be with you through everything. Don't be afraid."

Warm tears spilled over her lower lashes and chilled on her cheeks. Jack pulled off one of his gloves and reached for her, sliding his fingers into her hair and holding the back of her head. He bent down and kissed her deeply.

"We'll get through this together," he whispered.

Laurel leaned into his solid assurance. She lifted her arms around his neck and held his face to hers. "I can face anything if you're with me."

CHAPTER 15

With no outward struggle, Laurel went along with Agent Sanchez. Inside, her heart shattered. They killed her da. Jack was back in his role as a Federal Agent. She would go to jail.

Rick handcuffed her loosely, allowing her hands to hang in front of her for balance and they hiked up the mountain, through thick drifts of snow. Finally, they found the path the agents made coming in and they followed it to the base-camp.

On the hike back, Laurel grappled with the knowledge that her own father had wanted to shoot her—would have killed her—if Jack and his team hadn't intervened. The memory pierced her heart. A heavy ache flooded her chest. She hated him. And she loved him. She mourned him and was relieved he was dead. Her swirling emotions made her nauseous.

Once they reached the camp, Rick led Laurel to a large snowmobile and indicated that she could sit. When she did, he cuffed one of her hands to the machine. A medic tended to the wound on her thigh.

No stitches were necessary.

"We'll be heading down the mountain as soon as we can pack up the camp."

"That's fine."

Sanchez nodded once and went to help the squad stow their equipment.

Laurel watched the search and rescue team pack all their gear in an efficient maneuver, as if she were at the far end of a tunnel. Their voices sounded muted and distant. She closed her eyes against her roiling emotions. She pulled her knees up and rested her chin on them.

Jack brought up the tail end of the agent parade. He tied Wisaka to a tree on the outskirts of the camp and approached Laurel's side. "You doing all right?"

Laurel nodded. "I've been thinking about my da." She blinked rapidly, denying threatening tears. "He wanted to kill me." Laurel searched Jack's eyes as though he could give her an alternate truth, or soften the brutal reality.

"Roger wasn't in his right mind, Laurel. I don't think either of those men were." He reached for her hand. "I'm sorry about what happened to him."

Laurel's throat ached, but she had no more tears. "Me too." She caressed his knuckles with her thumb. "Is Jedediah going to live?"

"Looks like he'll make it long enough to face prosecution and go to prison."

"That's good, I guess."

"I guess. Frankly, I think the world would be a better place if he wasn't in it."

"What happens now?"

"We'll all head down to the compound on the snowmobiles. From there, the Bureau will airlift us to our different destinations. I think they'll take you to Coeur d'Alene where they'll process and question you in your initial interview."

"Will they arrest me?"

Jack looked down at his boots. "I hope not. I imagine they'll see you as a key witness and a crucial help to the police." He rested his hands on his hips and peered at her from under his lashes. His gaze pierced hers. "I don't know for sure what they'll to do, Laurel, but I'll be with you through it all, as much as I can, okay?"

"I'm not your responsibility, Jack." Her chest ached.

His bright blue eyes darkened with intensity and he raised his chin to look her directly in the eye. "What would you say if I told you I want you to be my responsibility?"

Laurel's heart kicked and her whole body warmed with his words. She brought his hand to her lips. "Thank you, Jack. You're sweet. I want that too, but first I need to be responsible for myself. It's about time, don't you agree?"

"I think you've done an amazing job being responsible for keeping your own mind amid years of attempted brainwashing and evil influence. The fact that Roger essentially kidnapped you and held you at a neo-Nazi compound wasn't your fault."

"The FBI may not see it that way."

Jack's gaze rested on her until she grew uncomfortable. "Just tell them the truth, Laurel. They'll understand."

Jack asked if he could be the one to bring Wisaka down the mountain, but after they gave him a preliminary medical examination at the camp, the

SAC ordered an agent to drive him back to the compound immediately for medical attention. Laurel lost sight of him once they were on the trail. She was cuffed and secured to the back of a snowmobile for the length of the trek with a group that took its time.

The agent she rode with was kind but professional. "I'll drive as smooth as possible, ma'am."

"Thanks. I'm sure I'll be fine."

"Sorry about the cuffs. Agent Stone asked me to take good care of you, but the bracelets aren't negotiable."

Laurel smiled, encouraged by the thought of Jack trying to look out for her. "I understand."

The ride was rough but much faster on the motorized skis. Laurel looked back for her horse and saw her with a woman she hadn't noticed before. The brunette walked with Wisaka behind a snowmobile fitted with a plow attachment and pulled a sled with a dog kennel on board. The plow knocked down some of the snow depth and made it easier for her mare to walk. It was a strange parade this group of people formed as they slowly descended the mountain. The entourage arrived at the compound late in the frozen afternoon.

Laurel complied with the directions of her guard as he led her to her temporary lock up. She was uncuffed and held in what used to be Jedediah Hotchkiss's personal library. The FBI tagged and confiscated the few books, Adolf Hitler's Mein Kampf among the prized tomes, as possible evidence. They left nothing in the room other than two matching upholstered chairs, and a side table with a lamp. The gun racks, shelves, and dry bar were empty.

Laurel paced the empty library like the cage it was. She hadn't seen or heard from Jack and she began to worry that he was more critically injured than she thought, or worse. Now that he was back among his fellow agents, warm, fed, and being cared for, he might have decided her problems took too much effort. Maybe, after seeing all the evidence of domestic terrorist plots, Jack figured she was far more trouble than she was worth. After all, she might spend years locked up in a federal prison. Besides, if, by the grace of God, the FBI released her, Laurel still had to find a way to get back to Scotland and her mother.

A knock sounded at the door a half-second before it opened. "Ms. MacNeil, we need to cuff you again. The chopper is here to fly you to the holding facility in Coeur d'Alene." The agent entered and Laurel held her arms together for him. The cuffs were cold and hung heavy on her thin wrists.

"Has Agent Stone sent me any word?"

"No, ma'am. I haven't heard anything."

"Do you know where he is? Is he okay?"

"I honestly don't know anything, other than that I am supposed to take you to the helicopter. Let's go."

"What about my horse? What will happen to her?"

"I don't know anything about that either, ma'am. Time to go."

Weight pressed in on her chest, making it hard to breathe. Laurel resisted the tears that wanted to form and bit down against her despair. Watching her father die and then losing Jack—it was all too much. There were so many things she wished she would have said—to both of them.

At the entrance to the helicopter, Laurel turned

around and scanned the compound hoping to get a glimpse of Jack or Wisaka. She found neither before the agent escorting her pressed on her back, nudging her into the transport. He gestured to a seat between two others and she took it.

Once the helicopter seats were full, the engines revved and the rotor blades turned, faster and faster. Within minutes, they were airborne. It was Laurel's first helicopter experience. She had pictured touring a tropical island if she ever rode in one. This was definitely not the makings of her fantasy.

As they swooped above the compound, Laurel finally caught sight of Jack. He stood with two other men who were not wearing the standard black FBI garb. Instead, both men wore blue jeans and heavy coats. The blond man held a cowboy hat in his hands. The other man was dark, like Jack, and rested a hand on Jack's shoulder. Jack pointed at the helicopter as it rose and the other men lifted their heads to look. They were strangers, yet somehow they seemed familiar to Laurel, and she tried to place them.

***

"They're taking her to the FBI Office in Coeur d'Alene to interview her. Depending on how that goes, they'll either incarcerate her or release her."

Jack's older brothers had arrived in Idaho hours after they heard he had gone missing. Rick told him they'd been prowling around demanding answers for the last couple of days. Their protectiveness reminded him of when they were young and they never gave him credit for being his own man. It also made him feel loved by a family he realized he didn't want to be without.

Trent, in his good-ole-boy fashion, grinned at Jack. "So, what you're telling us is that I missed my honeymoon to come track you down in the wild mountains of Idaho, only to find out you've been shacking up with some Scottish lass?"

Cade shook his head with mock indignation, though the sparkle in his dark eyes gave him away. "Should have known you weren't really lost—just on the hunt."

Jack let one side of his mouth curl and he regarded his brothers with affection out of the corner of his eye. "Yeah, the broken ribs and concussion were just a ploy to get into Laurel's cabin. It was all an elaborate ruse."

"Yep, I knew it." Trent laughed. "I taught this boy all the tricks in his book."

Cade clapped Jack on his bicep. "We're glad you're safe and sound man." A dark shadow seeped into his eyes, the gray turning slate. "I thought we'd lost you." The muscles in his jaw bulged.

"Thanks for coming out here, guys. Really. If they didn't find me, I would have wanted you guys out there. You two are the best trackers I know. Well, you and the dog."

"So where do you have to go next?" Cade turned to scan the compound grounds. "Are you finished here, or are there satellite groups you're investigating."

"We'll pass this case completely off to the Salt Lake Office and Homeland Security. I'm based in Chicago, so I'll probably return there."

Trent cocked his head and narrowed his eyes. "Won't you get some time off to recover? You ought to come home, to Stone Ranch, for a couple of months." He settled his cowboy hat on his head and propped his hands on his hips. "You need to heal, and besides, you promised Gran you'd be home for Christmas."

Jack met his brother's eyes. They were the same blue as his own—their mother's eyes. He favored Cade in looks, but Cade's eyes were slate. Trent was blond like their dad and granddad. He'd always stood out, though that was due more to his personality and over-the-top charm.

"That's true, I did." Jack nodded and stuffed his cold hands in his pockets. "Sorry I missed your wedding. I bet it was quite the spectacle," he teased.

"Is that a derogatory jab aimed at my wife? Cuz if it is, I'd be happy to finish breaking the few solid ribs you have left." Trent laughed.

"Seriously," Jack said. "I wish I could have been there."

"I know." Trent's gaze grew serious. Until several weeks ago, Trent and Jack had been estranged for over ten years. They were still finding their way back to brotherhood. "The ceremony was nice, of course, but I'll tell you what. I had the prettiest bride you've ever seen."

Cade shoved Trent's shoulder. "Not so fast, Romeo. Joscelyn is just as gorgeous, and you know it."

"Oh, my God. They're both beautiful. Don't start fighting over that." Jack laughed and then gripped his rib cage. "Shit. Laughing really hurts."

Kendra approached the brothers. "Agent Stone? I'm Kendra Dean. I'm with the K9 Search and Rescue Unit out of Denver. My dog, Baxter, helped to find you."

Jack stuck out his hand. "Nice to meet you, and thanks. Wasn't it you I saw leading the horse down from the mountain?"

"Yeah. I had horses growing up, so they tasked me. She did great though. Pretty mare." Kendra glanced at the corral where Wisaka stood. "What's the plan with her? My dog and I are flying back to Denver first thing in the morning."

Rick walked up the steps and joined them. "You have to leave so soon? Doesn't Baxter need a rest?"

Kendra glanced at Rick, a smile playing at the corners of her mouth. "He can rest on the plane."

"Who's gonna take care of the horse?" Rick shifted his weight.

"Not me. I was only told to get her down here safely." Kendra chuckled.

Jack walked to the end of the front deck and looked toward the corral at the side of the compound. "Did anyone feed her?"

Kendra answered, "Yeah, and I'll blanket her before I go, but I'm scheduled on the next chopper out of here."

"You're not even going to take me to dinner?" Rick teased. "After all we've been through?"

Kendra smirked and rolled her eyes. "Look me up next time you're in Denver."

"I'll do that." Rick held out his hand, and she shook it.

"So... the horse?" Kendra looked at Jack.

"I'll figure something out." Jack had no idea what to do with Laurel's horse now that she was on her way to Coeur d'Alene, but he'd come up with a plan.

"What horse are you guys talking about?" Trent

followed Jack's gaze.

Jack sighed. "Laurel owns that beautiful paint mare and I can't leave her here to fend for herself."

"Nope."

Cade popped the collar of his coat up on his neck. "Do they have a horse trailer around here somewhere?"

Jack asked a passing agent to check, and the man hustled toward the stable.

"We could haul her back to Trent's or my place and keep her until Laurel knows where she's going to land."

Jack nodded. "That'd be great. I've been ordered to go to the hospital in Spokane to get x-rays and see a doctor, but after that, I can probably get a few days to come back to Flint River and take care of things. By then I should have more information on what's happening with Laurel."

"It's settled then. If they don't have a trailer here, we can always rent one in Coeur d'Alene." Trent gripped the back of Jack's neck and gave him a brief hug. "Well, take care of it."

"Thanks guys. I think I forgot how good it is to have brothers."

"Damn straight." Trent laughed. "But don't get too mushy, it's totally self-serving on my part. When I tell Gran you're coming home, she'll start baking up a storm." He patted his belly.

Cade rolled his eyes and held his hand out to Jack. When he shook it, his oldest brother pulled him into a strong hug. "Call as soon as you talk to the doctor. I want to know you're okay."

"Will do."

CHAPTER 16

Laurel's helicopter ride was fairly short. She and a slight man covered in swastika tattoos were the only prisoners aboard.

"I heard you claimed to be my da when they caught you? Why?"

The man glared at her. When he spoke his words stumbled across a broken front tooth. "Tried to buy him and Uncle Jed more time." His lips twisted into a sneer. "I'm loyal. Which is a hell of a lot more than I can say about you."

Laurel dropped her head. Guilt over her father's death formed a cold knot in her chest.

"I heard you were the snitch." The man spit on the floor. A guard pushed him back with the butt of his rifle.

"I couldn't let children's lives be a means to an end. Even you have to agree that is pure evil." Laurel lifted her chin.

"Is what it is."

Laurel shook her head, filled with relief she would

no longer live with this type of mentality.

The FBI had flown Jedediah to Spokane, to the same hospital they took Jack to. The chopper landed at an Army base near Coeur d'Alene, where Laurel and the tattooed man rode in a jeep to the local FBI Field Office. By the time they finally arrived, it was well past midnight.

"Take the prisoners to their holding cells. We will begin interviewing in the morning." The agent who met them at the facility check-in point was old-school. He wore his hair clipped into a high-and-tight flat-top and he sported black, plastic-rimmed glasses. The white shirt under his suit-coat looked pressed even at this late hour and he had no humor or patience about him.

"Yes, sir," Laurel's guard responded. He gripped her upper arm and directed her down a long hallway. As he escorted the two detainees toward the lock-up wing of the facility, their shoes squeaked on the waxed, high-gloss floor. "There's no reason to be afraid, Ms. MacNeil. You'll be locked in your own cell until morning. The best thing to do is get some rest." Her guard opened a heavy metal door with a small square window cut into it at face height that led to a hall filled with cells. "Tomorrow's going to be a rough day."

"Thank you." Laurel murmured. *Thank you?* She couldn't believe she thanked her jailer. This was turning into a nightmare. One she had to face on her own.

Along what looked to be a brand-new hallway, the bright light gave the walls a pasty yellow tint. They passed several doors that had flip windows and slats cut into them that were bolted and locked shut. Her guard stopped at the fifth door on the left and turned the tattooed man over to two guards for processing. Laurel was directed to a room several doors further down.

"You'll be searched and then given prison clothes. A female guard will be here in just a minute."

Laurel nodded. Numbness crept into her bones, the whole situation was surreal. They waited for about twenty minutes before the large female guard showed up. The only words she spoke were commands to strip, where to stand, and a rote explanation of what she was doing during each part of the search.

After the humiliating experience of a strip search, Laurel dressed in what looked like orange medical scrubs.

"Take off your necklace and put it with your other personal affects." The guard ordered.

Laurel balked, and she clasped the sterling-silver thistle charm. "But, I never take this off."

"I'm not asking." The bull of a woman held out her hand waiting. Her scowl lines carved deep crevices in her face.

With trembling fingers and a lump in her throat, Laurel unclasped the chain, praying she would get the necklace back. She placed it in the large palm.

"Your intake officer is waiting for you in the hall."

Laurel opened the door and found the agent. He gestured for her to walk in front of him further down the hall. They went through another barricade and stopped at the first opening on the left.

"Welcome to the FBI's version of Motel 6." He unlocked and opened the heavy door.

Laurel peered in. There was a single cot with a

sheet and blanket neatly folded and sitting on top of a flat-looking pillow in the middle of the thin mattress. A stainless-steel commode and a small sink stood side-by-side in the corner. Nothing else. She'd been in worse. She took a deep breath and after glancing at the agent, she stepped inside. "Am I under arrest?"

"Not technically. We are holding you for questioning, after which we'll determine if we need to arrest you. Try to get some sleep." The guard said before he pulled the door closed. Laurel heard the bolt slide into place and the rattle of the lock.

Tears threatened. Laurel spoke out loud to herself. "No crying. Fretting and tears will serve no purpose whatsoever." Laurel threw her shoulders back and lifted her chin. She shook out the sheet and focused on making her bed.

The lights went out and Laurel laid on the bed in complete darkness. Sleep refused to join her in the jail cell. It seemed years later, when morning arrived, and the lights turned on with glaring accusation. Laurel rolled to her side and pushed herself off the cot. She stretched and attempted to freshen up at the tiny sink. There was no mirror or any way to tame her hair. Erratic energy bounced around inside her frame, so she paced to ease her tension as she waited for what the day would bring.

Before long, her guard from the night before opened the door. He followed her down the hallway and showed her to a plain room with a stainless-steel table in the middle and three chairs. A video camera was mounted near the ceiling in the upper right corner. Her guard pointed to the chair facing the camera.

"Please have a seat. Your interview agents will be

in momentarily."

Laurel pulled out the chair and sank onto it. "Excuse me, have you heard anything from Agent Stone?"

The guard kept his eyes on the file folder he held. "No ma'am. Sorry." He turned and left, closing and locking the door behind him.

Laurel folded her arms on the table and rested her head. Jack had been taken to the hospital. Her heart wrenched with worry that injuries were worse than they realized. What if after the exertion of saving her, the doctors found internal bleeding? What if Jack was fine and simply ready to settle back into his own comfortable life? Perhaps he wanted to forget all about her. Maybe she was just part of the job. Laurel let out a pain-saturated sigh.

She heard the metal clicking of the lock before the door swung open and two agents entered. A man and a woman both dressed in dark suits. The woman carried a file-folder.

"Ms. MacNeil, I am Special Agent Moon, and I believe you've met Special Agent Sanchez."

Relief, that Laurel refused to allow to become hope, poured through her. It was good to see a familiar face. A face that belonged to a man who would know something about Jack. "Yes, it's good to see you."

Agent Sanchez nodded, set a pink box on the table, and took his seat. "I trust they have treated you well?"

"Yes, fine." She bore into him with what she hoped was a meaningful stare. "Have you heard from Jack?"

Rick Sanchez was all business. "Yes. He has two

broken ribs and four fractures. He'll be in the hospital for a couple of days." He cleared his throat. "Now, let's get on with your interview."

"No other internal injuries?"

"No, he's going to be fine."

"Thank God." Laurel released a long breath. "Will you tell him I asked about him?"

Sanchez nodded.

Moon evened out her stack of papers with a sharp tap on the table. "Would you like a glass of water, Ms. MacNeil? We will be in here for the better part of the morning."

Laurel received the redirect for the slap it was. "No, thank you. I'm fine."

Agent Sanchez pushed the box into the center of the table. "Help yourself to a donut."

"No, thanks."

"Good," Moon snapped. "Now, just answer our questions honestly and to the best of your ability and we'll get through this as quickly as possible." Moon opened her file and picked up the first page. "Roger MacNeil was your father?"

"Yes." The pressure returned to her chest.

"How long have you been living in the United States of America?"

"About ten years."

"You are a British citizen?"

"Yes."

"Do you have a passport?"

"I had one to get here, but my father kept it. I don't know where. He may have destroyed it."

The questions droned on and on. They were the type of questions whose answers the agents already knew or could easily look up. Eventually, a guard brought lunch in. He removed the box of donuts and filled the small table with hoagie sandwiches and Cokes. After lunch, they lobbed the real questions at Laurel in rapid succession.

Yes, she knew that she lived inside a neo-Nazi compound. No, she couldn't leave at will, except to go to the cabin. Yes, she was held there, but where else would she go in a foreign country with no money and no ID? No, she had not had contact with her mother since she left Scotland. She didn't know if her mother knew where she was or if she was safe. She didn't believe her mother knew anything about the neo-Nazi movement.

Yes, Laurel knew about the bomb.

Two pairs of eyes stared at her. The silence was heavy and hot like a rough wool blanket.

Laurel explained that when she first heard about the plan to bomb a school, she listened closely and gathered as much information as she could. There was no way she could let something like that happen to innocent children—to their families. The bomber, Eugene Werner, was a favorite of Jedediah Hotchkiss and the man had his eye on Laurel. Werner wanted her and she used that to her advantage. He bragged to her about the bombing plot and willingly answered all her questions.

Once she had all the details, she stole her father's mobile phone and called the police to give them an anonymous tip. Laurel didn't know if her information helped or not until Jedediah threw a fit over the failed bombing and bank robbery. He and her father ranted for days.

When Hotchkiss and her da started to lose it after their spoiled mission, Laurel spent as much time as she could up at the cabin. She had thought the cabin was a place where she could be free. But when MacNeil almost shot her himself, Laurel realized it was more likely another form of captivity where he could murder her and leave her body where no one would ever find it.

Laurel replayed the events of Jack being shot in the chest and falling down the cliff of the ravine, of their time together in the cabin, the roof collapse, and the attack by Hotchkiss and her father. She spelled out everything she could remember up until the moment she met Agent Sanchez, leaving her feelings for Jack out of the story.

"And you know the rest from there," she concluded.

Moon made a note in the margin of her typed page. "I'm still struggling with the idea that you lived on this compound for ten years and never tried to escape."

"I didn't know where we were or how far we were from any civilized town. But, I did know the penalty for trying to run away was a month or more in solitary confinement in a pit underground, and whatever debasement the guards decided to put me through."

"What about when you were allowed to go up to the cabin? You had a horse, you could have escaped then."

Laurel's shoulders slumped. "Right. I could have. Or I could have at least tried, but I didn't. I guess, I felt free there and didn't feel the need to escape." She looked from one agent to the other and back. She grew tired of answering the same questions over and over. Exhaustion dragged at her body. Laurel rubbed her face with her hands. "So, what happens now?"

Agent Sanchez met her gaze. "Our superiors will go over your interview and decide whether there is enough evidence to arrest you and keep you in jail until the trial, or they may choose to put you up in a hotel near the district court. I don't think they'll find any cause for an arrest. But either way, you'll have to stay in the States until after the trial. Assuming they'll release you, you can apply for a U-visa."

"What is that?"

"A U-visa allows foreign victims of crime who meet certain requirements to stay in the United States. In your case, you're a witness, but you're more of a victim with the parental kidnapping and abuse. That's what may make you eligible." Agent Sanchez sipped the remainder of his drink.

"There are three requirements to qualify," he continued. "The first is a crime requirement, meaning that you are the victim of a crime. The second, is a helpfulness requirement, so you need to have helped either law enforcement or the prosecution." He reached for the paper sandwich trash and wadded it up. "Third, is a harm requirement, meaning that you suffered some sort of physical or emotional harm from the crime. Clearly, you've suffered harm, and you're willing to be helpful for the prosecution." He tossed the trash into a bin.

"Okay, but what would having a U-visa mean for me?"

"It provides a few benefits. You'd be allowed to live legally in the United States for four years, and after three years of having the U-visa, you can actually apply for a green card to stay here permanently." Pushing his chair back, Sanchez stood and brushed a few crumbs from his slacks.

"If you get a green card, you can go on to apply to become a U.S. Citizen. Also, with the U-visa, you get permission to work in the United States right away, so you can survive. Most other visa holders don't have this option." He pushed his chair back to the table. "It can take a while before you get approved, so I'll get you the application right away if you want me to."

"Thank you." Laurel's stomach turned in on itself. "What if I don't get approved?"

"Then you'll have to get a new passport from the British Consulate and return to Scotland without delay."

"What will I do until then?" Laurel stared at him in dismay.

"Let's just take one step at a time. I'll bring you an application this afternoon."

Agent Moon finished gathering her papers and stood. "District 9 Federal Court is held in San Francisco. We will fly you there and house you near the courthouse until you testify. Perhaps you'll hear early." She held out her hand and her smile was surprisingly warm. "Thank you for your statement and for answering our questions."

Surely Jack would have to testify. There was a good chance Laurel would see him before this was all over, before she returned to Scotland. "Have you located my mother?"

Moon shook her head. "Not that I'm aware of. Is her last name MacNeil as well?"

"It was when I left. I guess I don't know what all has happened in the last ten years."

As if on cue, the door opened and Agent Sanchez

reached for Laurel's hand and squeezed. "We'll let you know if we find anything out."

CHAPTER 17

L aurel sat in the District 9 Federal Courtroom wearing a mauve skirt-suit and practical shoes provided to her by the FBI. The suit was too big. The shoulder-pads drooped forward, and the skirt slid around when she walked so the zipper ended up in the front. Laurel fidgeted to keep the clothing parts in the right places. Her insides mimicked the disheveled wardrobe. She felt as out-of-place as she knew she looked.

Laurel wore her long, black hair smoothed into a chignon at the nape of her neck. Her fingers searched her throat where her Scottish-thistle pendant used to hang. It never made it into her envelope of personal items she left at the holding facility her first night in custody. She dropped her hand into her lap and held it there clasped in the other. The loss left a hole in her heart.

She sat in a chair positioned behind the wooden bar that separated the court from the gallery. Laurel sat to the back and right of the federal prosecutor, along with a handful of people whom she had lived with on the compound. She met their gazes straight on, but no one spoke to her. Fear and loneliness curled around her shoulders like an iron stole she couldn't shake off.

In the days following her interview, the FBI flew Laurel to San Francisco and housed her in a cheap, but clean motel to await the trial. She walked to a nearby library and with the help of the librarian learned how to search for her mother on the computer. She had had no luck so far, and Laurel didn't know what to expect after the trial was over. She didn't belong anywhere or to anyone. She had complete freedom, and that was scarier than anything else she faced.

A rich, tawny wood paneled the courtroom walls, and an elevated judge's bench stood at the front of the room, framed by both a United States flag and a California flag. Laurel rolled her lips in-between her teeth and bit down as she watched twelve jurors file in and take their seats in black leather-upholstered chairs in the jury box.

The side door of the courtroom opened, and a guard escorted Jedediah Hotchkiss inside. Jedediah shuffled in sporting the same orange prison clothing they had forced Laurel to wear during her brief time in jail. His arm, on the side of his chest and shoulder where he'd been shot, was in a sling, strapped against his body. His free hand was cuffed to a chain that ran around his waist and was connected to his shackled feet. The guard pulled out a chair next to the government-appointed defense attorney and clipped Hotchkiss's handcuffs to a bar attached to the table. He did not look at the crowd. He did not acknowledge any of his flock.

Laurel had never been inside a courtroom before and was caught up in the proceedings. She studied each juror as they watched Hotchkiss and wondered what they thought of him. Her gaze panned the faces in the room. She recognized a few of the FBI Agents. Jack was not among them. A cold weight pressed against her sternum and she turned to face forward.

The bailiff stood and sang out, "All rise. Federal District 9 Court of the United States of America is now in session, the Honorable Judge Turnbull presiding."

A serious man draped in black entered the courtroom from a door set in the wall behind the bench. He sat in the chair on the platform at the desk. "Are the prosecution and defense both ready to begin this trial?"

Both attorneys confirmed that they were.

"Very well. Everyone please be seated." The judge slipped on a pair of reading glasses and scanned a stack of papers on his desk. All the people sat with the exception of the federal prosecutor. The judge looked up and nodded at him. "You may begin your opening statement."

Laurel listened intently to the case put forth by the prosecutor. She agreed with all the facts he promised to present during the trial. It seemed the government knew everything that had ever happened in Jedediah Hotchkiss's life. Her chest constricted at the mention of her da's name, but she had no more tears for him.

The morning droned on as witness after witness confirmed the prosecutor's allegations with their testimonies. One of the heavy, wooden doors at the back of the room swung open and Laurel glanced at the movement. Jack entered the gallery. She sucked in a quick breath. He looked dashing in his dark suit and pristine white shirt, clean shaven, and with a fresh haircut. Laurel's mouth dropped open, and she stared.

Jack leaned into the guard standing by the door and whispered something. He panned the faces until he found hers. Their gazes snapped together, and she saw only him. The proceedings, the people, even the room itself faded away, and she smiled at him, lifting her fingers in a mute "hello".

His eyes sparkled under his dark lashes and he flashed a perfect white smile. They stared at each other saying nothing, saying everything. An objection was made and sustained. The defense attorney asked for a short recess. The judge granted it, and rose, followed by the crowd. When the people stood, Laurel lost sight of Jack for several seconds. Too long.

Laurel's part of the court proceeding lasted four days. She was not allowed to speak to Jack, or anyone, during that time, but she often caught him watching her. Jack sat in the back on the far side so they could see each other. Laurel tried to pay attention to the court. She knew she needed to follow what was going on, but all she could think about was the man sitting behind her.

She smiled at him and he winked. Sometimes his cheeks would deepen in color and he'd look down, smiling to himself. Encouraged, Laurel began to believe they might remain friends after all this was over.

The federal prosecutor had no interest in pursuing a case against Laurel or any of the other compound residents who had not taken part in major criminal actions and were willing to testify against those who had. His target laid squarely on the head of Jedediah Hotchkiss, since his cohort, Roger MacNeil, was deceased, and on anyone else who took an active role in illegal activity or domestic terrorism.

Eugene Werner, the attempted bomber in Chicago, had already been charged and faced a sentence of life without parole in a federal supermax prison. Though the bomb never went off at the school, it ended up killing two Chicago police officers along with Eugene's partners. He also murdered a man from Jack's hometown in cold blood purely because of the man's skin color.

Laurel was scheduled to testify on the same day as Eugene. The bailiff led him into the courtroom in chains and marched straight to the witness stand. A shudder of revulsion coursed through Laurel when Eugene grinned at her with his slick smile. She looked away and didn't cast her gaze in his direction again. Once loyal to Hotchkiss beyond reason, he was now equally vindictive. Werner's testimony alone could send Hotchkiss to death row.

The trial was expected to take about three weeks. They called Laurel to the witness stand to give her victim statement on the fourth day. She repeated the dark tale of her abduction and subsequent torture. The prosecutor asked her to recount how she learned about the plans for the bomb and what she did about it. Her voice rang over the speakers as the evidence of her 911 call was played for the court.

The defense attorney then took his turn pelting her with questions. He did his best to make it look as though Laurel was complicit in the bomb's planning, but his questioning fell short of his goal. After two long hours of giving her statements, Laurel was allowed to leave.

***

Laurel's emerald eyes sparked across the distance between them. The faint spray of freckles sprinkled on the pale skin of her nose and cheeks beguiled him. She was elegant with her hair pulled back, her slender neck graceful like a swan's. Jack wanted to climb over the seats to get to her, but he held himself in check. He closed his eyes in quick thanksgiving that Laurel made it through the legal proceedings. She was free to go. Jack followed her out the double doors into the hallway.

Laurel stretched out her hand toward him and he reached to grasp it. "Jack. I'm so glad you're here."

He pulled her into an embrace. "Are you okay? You've been treated well?" He buried his face in her hair and breathed in her scent.

"I'm fine… now." She clung tightly and smiled up at him. He wanted to kiss her, but held back. Now was not the time or place.

"Are you hungry? Can I take you to lunch?"

Laurel laughed. "I'd like that. I certainly don't have any other plans."

"We need to talk about that." Jack settled his hand on the small of her back and guided her out of the courthouse, through the throng of reporters and picketers, to a black Explorer. He helped Laurel into the passenger's seat and ran around to the other side. In minutes they were on the road away from the past.

"It's not every day we're in San Francisco. How

about we drive down the Wharf and have a seafood lunch?" He wanted to stare into those eyes, not watch the road, so he drove fast.

"Perfect. I don't care what I eat, I'm starved."

Jack ordered champagne to celebrate the future. He waited until the waiter opened the bottle and poured the twinkling liquid. He raised his glass to Laurel's. "Here's to your freedom and your future." He tapped her glass.

Laurel's face glowed. Her smile soft and full. "Slàinte."

Jack reached into an inside pocket of his suit coat. "I have something for you." He pulled out a handkerchief with his monogram hand stitched on the corner, folded around a hard object. He handed it to her.

Laurel's brow creased. "What is it?"

Jack's smile broadened. "Unwrap it and see."

She unfolded the linen and found her silver thistle charm inside. Wet, green eyes darted up to him. "Where did you find this? I thought I'd lost it forever."

"It was close. When they released me from the hospital in Spokane, I went down to the field office in Coeur d'Alene to catch up with you. You'd already flown to San Fran, but I passed a female guard in the hall and she was wearing your charm." Jack sipped his champagne. "When I confronted her, she caved. She took it off and begged me not to tell."

"Did you?

"Report her? Absolutely. But none of that matters. I know how much this necklace means to you." His chest glowed with warmth at the look in her eyes as she held the sterling thistle.

Laurel reached for his hand. "How can I thank you?" She dabbed a stray tear with the handkerchief and ran her thumb over the stitch-work.

"My gran made me a set. They're old fashioned, but I like them."

A wistful smile graced her mouth. "My mam tried to teach me needlework. I wish I would have tried harder."

"You'll have another chance." Jack squeezed her fingers. "Speaking of that, have you thought about your next step? What are you going to do now?" His gut churned, suddenly nervous, not knowing her plans.

Laurel's eyes flashed large, and she dropped her gaze to the bubbles lining her glass. She lifted it by the stem and took a sip. "Honestly, I have no idea." When she looked up, Jack lost himself in a sea of green.

She continued, seemingly unaware that he fought to focus on her words. "I've applied for something called a U-visa but I have to wait to hear if it gets approved. I'm not sure I want to stay in America, but I'd like to have the option."

"Not stay?" His brows pinched.

"I'm eager to go home and find my mother. I also have to figure out what to do with my horse. But, all of that takes money and I have none. I can get a job in America if the visa comes through." She took another sip, this one larger. "I do have thoughts for the distant future though. I think I'd like to go to school to become a nurse." Her eyes searched his.

He knew she needed understanding, even encouragement, but he tripped on the thought of her leaving.

"In a way, I feel like I've just been born. In many other ways, I feel stuck, and I'm not sure what I want to do."

Jack reached for her hand again. He yearned to chase away the fear hovering in her eyes, but it wasn't his place to take over her life. "Wisaka is fine. My brothers came to Idaho when they heard I was missing, and I got a chance to talk to them before my commander shipped me off to the hospital. They rented a trailer and hauled your horse to Trent's ranch in Flint River, Montana. She can stay there for as long as you need, so that's one thing off your plate of concerns."

"Thank you, Jack. That's so nice. I'll pay for her feed as soon as I earn some money." Her expression was so earnest, he cupped her cheek in his hand.

"It's not a problem. Trent has more hay than he can use. She is welcome, for however long you need—at no charge."

"Jack—"

He brushed past her objection. "You said you want to find your mom? Have you searched for her on the internet?"

"I've tried a little, but I'm so out of touch with all the new technology. I feel like I've lived in a cave for the last ten years." Laurel made a moue with her lips. "I suppose, in a way, I have. Would you help me?"

Pleased to be able to assist her in any way, Jack pulled out his phone and scooted his chair close to Laurel's so she could see the screen. Together, they began a search that would lead them on their next adventure.

CHAPTER 18

Over lunch that day, Laurel and Jack decided that her first step would be to go back to Stone Ranch with him. She could be with Wisaka and have a place to stay while she waited on the visa. Staying in Montana afforded her time to search for her mom and make plans for her future. Mostly, though neither of them said it, it gave them a chance to get to know each other outside of crisis.

Jack's brother, Cade, and his wife, Joscelyn, promised to pick them up at the airport in Missoula and drive them to Jack's family home. Laurel's stomach tightened as their plane descended and it bounced into her throat when they touched down. She was opening the door to an entirely new life and had no clue what she'd find on the other side.

Jack took her hand. "Everything's going to be all right."

Laurel nodded, but couldn't speak through her dry throat. Her tongue cemented itself to the roof of her mouth. She didn't know what she would do if she didn't have Jack in her corner, but the thought of meeting his family made her want to turn and run. What would they think of her—the daughter of a terrorist and an acquaintance of the man who murdered their friend? Laurel's stomach rolled. *I should have kept the motion-sickness bag from the airplane.*

When she and Jack exited the terminal, a big red pick-up truck pulled to the curb. The man driving looked like an older version of Jack, one who had seen more than his fair share of pain. The men had the same coloring and smile. A woman with blonde hair twisted into a long plait sat next to him. A gentle kindness shone in her eyes when she smiled at them. Laurel felt her skin relax and a few muscles in her neck released.

Hugs and introductions were quick since they had to pull away from the curb as soon as possible. Joscelyn turned in her seat to face Laurel and Jack in the back. "How was your flight? Are you guys hungry?"

Laurel shook her head and Jack answered, "The flight was smooth and we ate at the airport before we boarded. Let's just head home. I think Laurel would like to see her horse."

Joscelyn shifted her gaze to Laurel. "She's a beautiful paint. I bet you've been worried about her, but rest assured, Trent has taken great care of her and she's happily ensconced at Stone Ranch."

"I don't know how to thank everyone." Laurel swallowed. "You've all done so much for me and you don't even know me. Your family is grand."

The side of Jack's mouth curled up. "Wait till you meet our grandma Mary."

Laurel smiled at the obvious affection in Jack's

voice. "How far is the ranch from here?" Laurel peered out the window at the wide expanses of grassland that rolled in waves up to the base of tall, dark mountains.

Cade glanced at them in the rearview mirror. "It's about an hour, but I'll drive fast. Gran has been cooking all weekend, and she'll skin me alive if I don't get you two home straight away."

Joscelyn laughed. "Laurel, you're going to love Mary. She just sort of draws you in and makes you part of the family."

Laurel's stomach hardened, like a clenched fist. She didn't believe the Stones would accept her so openly, knowing who she was.

***

Jack gazed out the window at passing ranches poised against their blue-violet mountain backdrop. He'd been gone for ten years, but still he knew this land like he knew his own hands. It called to his soul, though he'd tried to ignore the siren song for years now. He looked forward to spending his rehab month in Montana, and he hoped he could heal the relationships with his family at the same time. They'd come a long way in the fall when he first came home, but he understood they needed more time before being together felt natural and comfortable, again.

Jack reached forward and gripped his brother's shoulder. "Thanks for hauling Laurel's horse home, Cade. She would have had to go to a shelter or something if you guys hadn't stepped in. I really appreciate it."

Cade nodded then winked at Laurel in the

rearview. "What are big brothers for if not to bail their baby brothers out of jams?"

Jack chuckled, glad for a noise he could make that could wiggle around the stone in his throat.

"Don't think Trent isn't looking for a way to benefit though." Joscelyn grinned. "He's already considering a breeding program between his stallion, King, and your mare."

"Is he?" Laurel sputtered.

"Yeah, and I have to admit, I agree they'd make terrific babies. Wisaka is absolutely gorgeous and wait until you see King. He's a big, beautifully built, sorrel quarter-horse." Joscelyn reached to touch Laurel's knee. "Don't worry, he'll discuss his thoughts with you before he does anything. He's been careful to keep his stallion away from your mare for the time being."

Laurel glanced at Jack and he noted the fear lurking in her eyes. She wiped her hands on her thighs and swallowed.

Jack clasped her hand. "Hey, everything will be okay. We'll take it slow. You don't have to make any decisions about anything until you're ready. I promise."

Laurel nodded and Jack saw the glint of tears before she turned her gaze out the window.

Joscelyn dropped her tone to a soothing timbre. "Jack's right, Laurel. I'm sorry. I'm excited that you're here, but I should have been more sensitive. You've been through so much in the past several weeks. We'll get you home and bundle you up in front of the fireplace and pamper you. You don't have to think about anything, at least for a while. And when you're ready, we are all here to support you."

Laurel faced Joscelyn, her voice tight with anguish. "Why are you all being so kind to me? I can't bear it. I've had losses, but so have you, and it's because of people like my da." Her throat trembled. "Your friend didn't deserve to die."

Warmth spilled out of Joscelyn's eyes. "Laurel, you are as much a victim of the situation as anyone. No one blames you. In fact, you are a hero. Wasn't it your phone call to the police that prevented the children in Chicago from being hurt? And though your father was caught up in some awful things, he was still your father. You need to grieve his loss. We understand that and want to support you." Joscelyn rested her hand on Laurel's knee. "I'm here if you'd like to talk, or if you just want to go on a long ride in silence. What's important for you to understand is that you're not alone."

Jack didn't know his brother's new wife well, but he was grateful for her in that moment.

Laurel's tears made good on their threat to fall and she wiped at her cheeks with her sleeve.

Cade reached in his pocket and handed Laurel a bandana over the back of the seat before changing the subject. "Looks like you're gonna be home for Christmas, Jack. Gran is as happy as punch."

Jack caught Cade's eye in the mirror and held it in silent gratitude. "Nothing like a Flint River Christmas, that's for sure. It's been too long."

"It has, but that's all in the past now." Cade pointed out their small hometown on the left as they passed by.

Thirty minutes later, they pulled into the winding drive toward their family's ranch. Jack's chest expanded against the bandages taped to his ribs when he saw Mary, Sadie, and Trent with his arm around Tonya, standing out in the cold on the porch waiting for them. Laurel gripped his hand so tight his knuckles crunched together, her pulse taking off like a jet.

CHAPTER 19

Laurel had never been around a family like this. Her first sixteen years she had only her mam and grand-da until he passed on. Then everything fell apart and her father came to get her. She didn't have any extended relatives that she knew about. Both her parents were only-children.

When Cade parked the truck, Jack's grandma ambled down the steps of the white farmhouse porch. She made a beeline for Laurel's door. With a quick glance at Jack for reassurance, Laurel reached for the handle. The size and forthrightness of Jack's family overwhelmed her. Her heart lurched and stuttered before she drew a fortifying breath.

Joscelyn beat her out of the truck. "Hello, Mary." She pulled the older woman into an embrace effectively giving Laurel the space she needed to breathe. She kept her arm around Mary while she introduced her. Jack's grandma must have taken the hint since she held her hands together and didn't immediately pull Laurel into her arms.

"Hello, Laurel, dear. Welcome, welcome. We're so happy to have you here—you *and* Jack." The woman's loving gaze rested on her youngest grandson. Jack kissed her cheek and hugged her tight. "Oh, be careful of your ribs." Mary pulled back and gently placed her hands inside the front of Jack's coat on his ribcage.

"I'm fine, Gran. Please don't fuss."

Mary gave him a mock glare. "You boys, always trying to be so tough. You're not fine. You have broken bones."

***

With Tonya's hand in his, Trent approached Jack. "He's fine, Gran. Don't baby him. I need help re-stacking hay in the barn this afternoon and I don't want to have to hear him whining."

Jack's chest warmed and the tension in his neck and shoulders relaxed with the friendly teasing. If Trent didn't give him crap, then he'd know things were still bad between them. As it was now, he had hope. "I'm not helping you in the barn. It's not my fault you didn't stack the hay right the first time."

Trent's eyes gleamed, and he reached for the back of Jack's head, pulling him into a quick man-hug and a pat on the shoulder. "Good to have you home, little brother."

"Good to be here." Jack turned to Tonya. "Tonya, you get prettier every time I see you. What are you doing with this guy?"

Tonya's soft laugh was lost in Jack's shoulder when they embraced. "Welcome home, Jack. I hope you'll be here for a very long time."

"We'll see. I don't know what the future holds at this point." Jack put his arm around Laurel and nudged her forward into the group. "Everyone, this is Laurel MacNeil."

Trent nodded but his grip on Tonya's shoulders tightened. "Hey." The lack of enthusiasm in the greeting thickened the air around them.

Sadie broke the tension and stepped forward to shake Laurel's hand. "Hi, I'm Sadie. Cade's... well, Cade and Joscelyn's daughter." She paused to smile at her new step-mom. "Your horse is so amazing. What kind of riding do you do with her?"

A ghost smile flitted across Laurel's lips. "Just trail riding. Will you take me to see her?"

"Sure." Sadie linked her arm through Laurel's and led her toward the barn, chatting about horses the whole way.

Jack turned back to Trent. "Hey, man. Do you have a problem with Laurel?"

Trent cast his eyes down. "No, not really."

Tonya looped her hand through the crook of Trent's elbow. "To be honest, Jack, it's kind of awkward, you know? She comes from the cult of people responsible for Matthew's death. He was our friend and a good man. It still hurts."

Trent met Jack's eye. "We realize it wasn't Laurel's fault, but her being here brings up a lot of pain and bad memories."

Tonya leaned into Trent's shoulder. "And Jack... you should be aware that Laiken Jefferson, Matthew's daughter, is in town dealing with her dad's estate. We just got back from seeing her."

Joscelyn touched Jack's arm. "There's strong emotions going on inside of everyone right now, but if I know this family, given a little time, we'll work through them all and be stronger for it."

Jack nodded, his own conflicting emotions clogging his airway. He wanted to leap to Laurel's defense, but he also understood, Trent had always been close to Matthew. Even as a kid. And poor Laiken. She'd been in his grade at school and they'd been pals. "A bunch of serious shit has gone on over the past several months. There's no denying that."

Mary clapped her hands together. "Yes, Jack, that's true. So now, we need to get inside where it's warm, eat some good food, relax, and start healing. Right Joscelyn?"

Joscelyn squeezed Mary's shoulders. "I couldn't have said it better myself." Her smile was broad and the kind eyes that sought Jack's brimmed with compassion.

***

Dinner consisted of Mary's famous peppery chicken-fried steak, mashed potatoes slathered with a rich brown gravy, green beans baked with bacon, and homemade bread drenched with butter and honey. The food saturated the room with a delectable aroma and Laurel ate more than she had in what seemed like months. It was a pure joy to sit around a table with a bunch of people whose love was obvious in their banter and teasing. Laughter danced in the evening air.

After dinner, the family drew Laurel into the fold and treated her like one of their own. Even Trent offered an olive branch in the form of a dishtowel and a crooked grin. She helped with the dishes and clean-up, grateful for their acceptance. After she dried the last plate, and hung the tea-towel, Laurel heard tires crunching in the snow outside.

Jack stood to the side of the window and peered out. "You expecting someone?"

"Nope." Trent rose and went to open the front door. His face was grim as he turned back to the family. "It's Laiken and her grandpa. Did you know they were coming out here tonight, Gran?"

Mary let out a heavy breath. "No. No, I didn't, but they're always welcome. Invite them in for dessert."

Trent and Jack shared a long look before Trent stepped out onto the porch. Laurel felt the tension, but didn't understand why its presence laid heavy in the room. She moved to where Joscelyn cut a chocolate-raspberry cake at the table. "What's going on? Why is everyone acting strange?"

Joscelyn laid down the knife and wiped her fingers on a dishcloth. "Laiken is Matthew Jefferson's daughter. Matthew was the man Eugene Werner murdered." A wash of nausea coursed through Laurel's belly and her head swam. Joscelyn took her hand. "No one blames you for what happened, but it might be uncomfortable for Laiken, knowing you were connected to the same group Werner came from."

"But—"

"I know, Laurel." Joscelyn set a reassuring hand on Laurel's shoulder. "Everyone knows you had no part in Matthew's death. Still, this will be hard. I'm right here though. We'll get through this together, one step at a time. Okay?"

Laurel nodded, briefly wondering if this was what

it was like to have a sister, or even a good friend. It had been a long time since she had felt close to another woman. Her stomach balled up tight when footsteps sounded on the porch. Laurel heard Trent's deep voice, but couldn't hear his words. The door opened and Laurel gripped Joscelyn's hand fiercely.

Trent held the door for his friends. "Come on in. Gran made a chocolate cake and you know she won't let you out of here until you've a piece."

Laurel had never seen an African-American person. She'd been completely isolated at the compound and before that she lived in Scotland. There, she'd known dark-skinned people, but they'd had Indian or Middle-Eastern heritage. The young woman standing before her, though her eyes held a deep grief, was utterly beautiful. The older man with her also carried heavy sorrow in the lines around his dark eyes and mouth, but he smiled at each person in the room.

His eyes rested on Mary. "Well, now, no one will ever be able to say I missed out on a chance to enjoy a piece of Miss Mary's cake." His eyes twinkled around the pain anchored at their center.

"Oh, Elijah, you're still as full of nonsense as you always were." Mary stood and held her hands out to the man. "I hate the circumstances, but it sure is good to see you, you old coot." Mary's skin glowed a lovely rose as she embraced her friend. "How are you holding up, Laiken? Do you need any help at your dad's shop or his house? I have three strong boys here at the moment, who I know would be happy to lend a hand."

Laiken slid into Mary's embrace and rested there for a while, accepting comfort before she raised her head. "No, I don't think I'll need help. In fact, that's why we stopped by. I have some news." Her dark eyes took in each face before landing on Laurel.

Laurel's head swam, and she swallowed, but her throat had become the Sahara and stuck to itself. Joscelyn must have sensed her sway because she put an arm around Laurel's waist and gave her a squeeze.

"Laiken, it's a pleasure to meet you. I'm Cade's wife, Joscelyn. I've heard a lot about you and your family. I'm so sorry about your dad."

Laiken's gaze flickered to Joscelyn and then slid back to Laurel. "Thank you," was all she said. Laurel couldn't read the emotion behind her eyes.

Joscelyn continued, "This is Laurel MacNeil. She's a friend of Jack's."

Laiken's eyes narrowed slightly, and she lifted her chin a fraction. "I know who you are."

Tears flooded Laurel's eyes and guilt wrapped around her chest like the coils of a python, constricting her ability to breathe. Her body swayed into Joscelyn.

Jack rushed to her other side. "Let's get you a chair. Are you all right?"

Laurel wished she was anywhere else, but she knew she had to face this woman. The cold-blooded murder of her father was horrifying and though Laurel had no part in it, she felt as if she did. "Laiken, Mr. Jefferson," Laurel cleared her throat and forced strength into her voice. "I am beyond sick about what happened to your father. I'm terribly sorry. I know my being here probably causes you even more pain. I would have left if I knew you were coming. I'll leave now so you can enjoy your time with the Stones." Laurel pulled away from Jack and Joscelyn and stood before Laiken. The young woman stood two or three inches taller and Laurel looked up into her ebony eyes. "I simply can't express how sorry I am." Laurel turned to leave.

Laiken stuck out a hand to stop her, her voice low and liquid. "Trent explained to me you were basically a prisoner at that compound. That your father kidnapped you from your mother and held you there. You're a victim too. I don't blame you. I just hope you didn't learn the hate and bigotry they preached."

Laurel stared back at Laiken, baffled at the genuine offer of such grace. "I did my best to stay away from the others. My mother never hated anyone, and I tried to hold on to that."

"And you found a way to warn the FBI about the bombing. That was brave."

Laurel felt heat rush up her neck and into her face. "It wasn't brave. Brave would have been facing my father and staying on the phone-line so the police could track the call."

"Maybe. But you might have ended up dead." Laiken touched Laurel's shoulder. "Listen, we all do the best we can. I get that." Her eyes glistened with sudden tears. "Sometimes, life just really sucks."

Laurel nodded. "Aye, it does." She glanced at the others in the room, all staring at Laiken and her. "And sometimes it surprises you with unexpected blessings." She offered a wobbly smile.

Laiken gave her a nod. She turned to Jack. "So what's going to happen to Hotchkiss?"

Jack placed a reassuring hand on Laiken's shoulder. "The trial will last for another week, or so, but he'll most likely be convicted of conspiracy to commit a terrorist act upon innocent civilians on U.S.

soil, conspiracy to commit murder, federal hate crime charges, and child abduction charges."

Laiken's brow furrowed. "Child abduction? Do you mean Laurel?"

"No, that charge would have been against her father. But there's enough evidence that Hotchkiss took runaways back to the compound with him and then didn't allow them to leave. Eugene Werner was one such kid."

Laiken's eyes widened, and she returned her gaze to Laurel. "The whole thing is awful."

"Yes, it is. The good news is that Jack and the FBI have rescued the children that were living there. Now they have a chance to learn a better way of looking at the world."

Laiken smiled at her then, and Laurel warmed with hope.

Jack slid his arm around Laurel's shoulders and she drew in his strength. He said, "It's good to see you, Laiken. My gran is right. We'd be more than happy to help you with anything you need, but for now let's get that dessert served up. It's been years since I sank my teeth into Gran's chocolate-raspberry cake."

Elijah rubbed his hands together. "Hear, hear!" He held his elbow out for Mary to take, and he escorted her across the room to the table.

Trent touched Laiken's arm. "When you got here, you said you had some news?"

Laiken smiled. "Yes. Grandpa and I have decided to stay in Flint River and keep my dad's shop open. I think it's what he would have wanted."

"That's terrific. Good for you two." Trent hugged Laiken and everyone cheered.

Joscelyn went back to cutting the cake and slowly, the conversation started up and chugged along at a comfortable hum. Trent teased Sadie about a boy she mentioned and Cade glowered at her, causing her to giggle. Tonya shoved Trent's arm playfully. Mary seemed shy in the glow of Elijah's attention and the death grip around Laurel's lungs slowly loosened.

Jack stood behind Laurel. He placed his hands on her shoulders and pulled her back into his solid chest, whispering in her ear. "Well done. I know that was hard, but you're through the tough part. I'm proud of you."

Laurel closed her eyes. She wanted to stay here, in Jack's embrace and that of his wonderful, warm and welcoming family forever. But she was also desperate to start the search for her own.

CHAPTER 20

The next morning, Jack woke in his boyhood bedroom, to the scent of strong coffee and bacon. He lay in the too-small bed, his feet hanging off the end, and soaked in the sensations that came with a tapestry of memories. After a powerful stretch, he got out of bed, threw on his jeans and a shirt, and went in search of the dark roast.

"Good morning, Gran." He kissed his grandmother on the cheek before reaching for a mug. "Nothing like waking to one of your breakfasts on the ranch."

"You could do that every morning if you wanted to." Mary glanced at him out of the corner of her eye. "I do wish you'd stay home."

"I know Gran, but I have a job. At least I'll be here until the first of the year."

"Yes, and I'm glad to have you, I just wish it wasn't because you were hurt. I don't like the idea of you being an FBI agent."

Jack chuckled. "You didn't like me being in the

Army either, Gran, but a man has to do what a man has to do."

"That's nonsense. There's plenty around here for a man to do."

Trent's voice sounded from the stairwell as his boots clomped down the steps. "Nah, Gran—the work around here is for *real* men. There's no glamor or heroics—just dirt, sweat, and manure." He winked at Jack.

"Lots of manure—that's for sure," Jack scoffed playfully.

"How'd Laurel sleep? It was an intense night for her, having to face Laiken and all." Trent poured a cup of coffee and kissed Mary's cheek. "Morning, Gran."

Mary waved her spatula. "Good morning, good morning. Go sit. Pancakes are just about ready."

Jack drew a chair out from the table and slid into it. "I haven't seen her yet this morning. She handled the whole thing well though, I thought. Laiken too. Lots of grace there."

"Laiken's always been like that though. She learned that from Matthew." Trent carried his mug and the plate of bacon to the table. "God, I miss him." He sat at the head.

Tonya came down the stairs next. She wore one of Trent's shirts and her hair was still mussed from sleep. She looked like Marilyn Monroe just getting out of bed and Jack grinned. She looked adorable. It surprised him it took his brother as long as it did to stake his claim on her. He was damn lucky she'd waited around. "Mornin' Ton."

"Yes—it is." She made a face at him and continued on a beeline for the coffeepot.

Laurel was the last down, but she had showered and dressed for the day, her black hair still damp, but shining. "Breakfast sure smells grand, Mary. Thanks."

"Sit down and fill your plate." Mary held a platter loaded with pancakes in one hand and balanced four pancakes on her spatula in the other. She placed those on the plate in front of Laurel.

"Oh, I can't eat that much. Jack, you take two of those." Laurel pulled out her chair.

Jack reached for the top two only to have his hand swatted with Mary's kitchen wand. "Don't you touch those. There's plenty for you. Laurel, you need to gain your strength back. You've had a hard time. Now sit down and eat. Coffee?"

"Yes, please. But Mary, I really can't—"

"I wouldn't argue with her, Laurel. She has a mean streak." Jack rubbed his hand where he'd been smacked as though it really hurt.

"That's right and don't any of you forget it." Mary chuckled on her way back to take command of the griddle.

***

After breakfast, Trent and Tonya headed off to work and Mary busied herself in the kitchen preparing for dinner later. Jack sat next to Laurel in front of the computer in Trent's ranch office. "Where did you live when your dad came to get you?"

"Aberfeldy, in Perthshire." She scooted her chair closer as Jack typed the words into the search bar.

"Small town."

"Mmm-hmm."

"The Dewar's Distillery is there? That's cool."

"Yeah, it's the first scotch I learned to drink." Laurel smiled but her thoughts were far away.

"Do you have good memories?"

"I do. I miss Scotland. It's a lot greener than here."

"It looks beautiful." Jack clicked several links. "Look at that castle."

"There are castles everywhere."

Jack turned to look at Laurel. "Really?"

"Aye, there's so much history. I remember not appreciating that fact in school though." She grinned. "Too many dates to memorize."

They spent the morning searching for Laurel's mother. She remembered her mother had been a waitress at a pub when Laurel was young. She and Jack had some luck but also found a bit of mystery when they came across the Schiehallion Hotel. The name sounded familiar to Laurel, so Jack called, putting the phone on speaker.

They were told that Elspeth MacNeil had worked as a waitress there for almost fifteen years, up until about two months ago. The manager told Jack that Elspeth had called him and quit her job over the phone, giving him no notice. He had no idea where she was now. Concern gave weight to the man's voice as he explained that Elspeth had always been reliable and rarely asked for time off. Quitting in that manner was completely out of her character.

"Had she been acting differently before she quit?" Jack asked.

"No, not that I noticed, but she did have a long chat with one of the dinner guests about a week before she left us." The manager said he saw them talking again in the car park after the restaurant closed. "They were still there when I locked up and left for home."

"Was the guest male or female? Can you give a description?"

The manager told Jack he had never seen the man before. "It was dark and I don't really remember much, but I think he drove a black Land Rover."

"Okay. Do you have a recent address and phone number for Elspeth?"

"Hold on." The manager rummaged and came back on the line. He gave Jack the most recent information he had. "I've tried this number a time or two, though. There's never an answer."

"I appreciate your help. If you do hear from Ms. MacNeil, will you please tell her that her daughter, Laurel, is looking for her?"

"Her daughter, ye say?"

"Yes."

"Aye, will do. I hope you find her. If you do, won't ye tell her we miss her here at the Schiehallion."

"I will. Thank you." Jack ended the call.

"How will we ever find her now?" Laurel propped her arm on the desk and rested her chin in her hand.

Jack reached over and rubbed Laurel's back, easing her stiff muscles. "First, we'll try to contact the landlord of her last residence, but honestly, Laurel, it would be a lot easier to trace her if we went to Scotland."

Laurel sat up and blinked at Jack. "We?"

A sly smile crept across Jack's mouth. "Well, if you *want* me to come with you, that is."

A bubble of joy filled Laurel's chest and she sprang up from her chair and threw her arms around

Jack's neck. "I would love that." She wilted as fast as she bloomed. "But, how will I get there? I have to wait for the British Consulate to send me my new passport. Plus, I shouldn't leave until I hear back about the U-visa." Laurel flopped back into her chair. "I was hoping I'd find my mother and that she could help me pay for an airline ticket."

"I've been trying to get your visa expedited. But I have no pull on your passport since it comes from London. It shouldn't be a big deal though since you had one in the past, it just needs to be renewed. As soon as it's approved, they'll send it here. Hopefully it will arrive in early January. As far as getting a plane ticket—I can manage that."

"No, Jack. I can't let you pay for my ticket."

"You can pay me back later, besides you're low on options."

"No. That's far too generous." Laurel's brows drew together.

"Maybe the Bureau could help with expenses, since you're the victim of a crime inside the US. Let me see what I can find out." Jack smiled with exaggerated innocence.

Laurel saw through his ruse. She figured the agency wouldn't assist in travel expenses and that Jack planned to pay for her ticket secretly. He may be an amazing federal agent, but he was a terrible liar.

The following week, Mary brought a piping-hot chicken pot-pie with a flaky, buttery crust to the table. After everyone was served, and Trent gave the blessing, Jack cleared his throat.

"I wanted to let you all know, the Hotchkiss trial ended today. With all the evidence against Jedediah

Hotchkiss, the jury took a mere forty-five minutes to determine him guilty on all counts. The judge sentenced him to the federal death penalty. He'll be put to death via lethal injection within the month."

"Well, that's good news." Trent met Jack's eye.

"Yeah. I didn't figure it would go any other way, but it's a relief the whole thing is over." Jack took a long sip of water. "On another note, I want you all to know that as soon as Laurel's paperwork comes through, I'm going to take a leave of absence and fly with her to Scotland. I'm going to help her find her mom."

Three pairs of eyes stared at them. Mary spoke first. "When? You promised you'd be home for Christmas."

Trent sat forward in his chair. He covered their grandmother's hand with his and narrowed his eyes at Jack. "When?"

"Don't worry, Gran." Jack raised a hand and was quick to answer. "I *did* promise you, and we will stay here through the holidays, if that's okay with Trent and Tonya."

Trent sat back with a shrug. "Where else would you stay? Of course it's okay. This is your home."

Jack gave him a nod. "Thanks. We want to be here for Christmas, and we still have to get Laurel's documentation in order. We can't fly to Scotland until all that's settled."

Laurel picked up her fork and speared a juicy piece of chicken and some golden crust. She sopped it in gravy. "There's something mysterious going on with my mam. She seems to be missing and no one we talked to knows where she went." Laurel glanced at Jack. "Jack's promised to help me find her."

"If anyone can track her down, Jack can." Trent said before shoveling a large bite of the casserole into his mouth.

CHAPTER 21

On Saturday, Joscelyn and Tonya convinced Laurel to let them take her shopping.

Tonya walked Laurel to the floor-length mirror in her and Trent's bedroom and stood next to her. "It's sweet that you haven't complained about the clothes the FBI gave you from their victims care closet, but honestly, none of it fits very well."

Laurel stared at herself in the reflection and ran her hands over the baggy Seattle Seahawks sweatshirt. "It's fine. I mean, once I get a job, I'll get some different things, but..."

"You can't wait until you get a job. You'll need to have something with style to interview for a job in. Plus, a girl wants to feel beautiful. Do you feel beautiful in that man's sweatshirt?"

Laurel laughed. "It's warm."

Tonya rolled her eyes. "So is a sleeping bag, but you don't want to wear one around." Tonya opened her closet doors. "You're taller than I am, but I'm sure I have a top you can wear. Don't borrow anything from Joscelyn though or you'll end up looking like a rodeo queen."

"I heard that." Joscelyn entered the room and winked at Laurel.

Without missing a breath, Tonya hollered from inside, "Good. It's time you got a few new things too." Tonya came back out of the closet with several items draped over her arm. "Today, we're going to go shopping and have a beauty day." She held two tops up to Laurel and shook her head. "Laurel, you've never had the chance to find out what you like—what your style is. And we're going to help you." She glanced at Joscelyn and grinned. "Well, *I'll* help you, and Joscelyn can come along."

Joscelyn laughed. "Be careful, Laurel, Tonya can be a bit of a whirlwind. I'll help you stay strong."

Laurel wasn't sure how to handle Tonya. "Honestly, you're so kind, but I don't have any money to go to the shops with."

Tonya smirked. "I have Jack's credit card and he has plenty of money. He told me to go crazy."

"He did not." Laurel laughed.

"Okay, well maybe not in those words. He said something boring like 'Get whatever she needs.'" Tonya winked. "But he *meant* go crazy."

Sadie popped her head through the door. "Can I come?"

"Absolutely." Tonya reached for her hand and pulled her into the room. "I need all the help I can get."

***

That night, Mary announced that Elijah was

taking her out for dinner and the boys were on their own.

A wicked gleam swirled in Trent's eyes. "Gran, are you going on a date with that old codger?"

Mary's cheeks flamed. "I am just having a meal with an old friend."

"He's driving out here to pick you up?" Jack joined in. "Taking you to a restaurant? Sounds like a date to me."

Trent stood to look out the window at Elijah's approaching car. "He didn't ask my permission to take you on a date."

Cade came out of the kitchen with a beer. "I don't know, Gran. You hardly even know that old coot."

Mary swatted Trent with her purse. "I don't need your permission, and for your information, I have known that *old coot* since we were in the first grade."

"Back in the one-room schoolhouse?" Trent teased.

Mary pursed her lips at him.

A knock sounded at the door and Jack sprang to answer it. "Good evening, Mr. Jefferson. What can we do for you?"

Elijah's gaze moved from Jack to his grandmother, then took in his brothers. He removed his hat. "Good evening Jackson. Boys." He nodded to Cade and Trent. "I am here, with your permission of course, to take your lovely grandmother on what I hope to be the first of many dinner dates."

Both Jack and Trent were at a loss for words and Cade burst into laughter.

Trent recovered himself and shook Elijah's hand. "Have fun, you two. Don't stay out too late. Mary has a curfew, so have her home by ten."

Jack kissed Mary's reddened cheek and whispered, "Have a nice time, Gran." After the door closed behind her, he turned to his brothers. "Gran looked like a nervous girl going on her first date."

Cade tossed him a beer. "Good for her."

Jack caught the bottle, twisted off the lid, and went in search of a deck of cards. "Let's get our poker night going." Finding a deck on the bookshelf, he sat and shuffled. "What are we using for chips?"

"When did the girls say they'd be home?" Cade tossed a beer to Trent and went to the kitchen for snacks.

Trent opened a drawer and took out a box of poker chips. "With Tonya running the show? They won't leave Missoula until the last shop closes. I'm guessing they'll be home around ten."

Jack grinned. "Just enough time for me to take all your money."

A car pulled up out front and a minute later the door opened. Laurel stepped in, followed by the Stone women. When Jack saw her he stood so fast he knocked his chair over. Trent stood too.

"Sit down, Trent." Jack said, his eyes never leaving Laurel, his voice conveying awe for the woman standing before him.

"Are you kidding me? Four gorgeous women walk into my home and you expect me to sit down? You must not have listened well to the man who raised us."

Cade rose to his feet too, and took a step toward Joscelyn. "Wow. If this is what happens when you ladies go shopping, I guess we'll have to have poker night more often." He kissed his wife and then appraised his daughter. "You look beautiful, Sadie. You're grounded until you're thirty."

"Dad!" Sadie said in mock horror before she laughed.

Tonya practically bounced over to Trent. "We had a makeover day." She turned back to Laurel. "Take off your coat, honey. Let that boy see your new style." She clasped her hands in front of her mouth.

Laurel slipped her coat off and took a step forward. Jack couldn't speak. She spun around, her long dark hair, having been shaped at the ends, lifted like a silk curtain as she twirled. He'd never seen her with make-up before and she didn't need it, but he had to admit the light hints she applied tonight highlighted her natural beauty. Over tight blue jeans and ankle boots, she wore a blouse of blues and greens, threaded through with silver, that made her eyes dance in the light. When she faced him again, it was with an expression that hovered between wonder, magic, and hope.

"My God, Laurel. You're stunning." Jack shook his head. "I mean you're always beautiful, but you're... you..."

Laurel let out an excited laugh and ran to his arms. "I feel like Cinderella."

"You're a hell of a lot prettier than Cinderella."

Cade winked at Trent. "It's late. Time for me to get my girls home."

Tonya took Trent's arm and followed them to the door. "On that note, I offered to let Laurel use the apartment over my shop until she goes to Scotland. I thought she might like her own space while she's figuring things out."

Jack kissed Laurel behind her ear and whispered.

"Any chance you're ready to move in there tonight?"

***

Later, after Mary got home and everyone went up to bed, Jack and Laurel sat on the sofa in front of a quiet fire. She leaned against him and nestled into the crook of his arm. They sipped scotch and watched the flames flicker in its amber reflection.

"I had such a fun time today. I've never done that—spent an entire day shopping and going to the salon. The girls all treated me like…"

"Like family?" Jack kissed her temple.

Contentment filled her so full she thought she would burst with joy. "I want this to last forever." Laurel adamantly pushed her worry over her mother down deep inside herself not wanting to acknowledge her fear or the questions that came when she was alone.

***

Jack took Laurel's hand. "Going to Scotland will give us time and space alone together to figure out what the future holds for us." He held his breath and looked at her through the corner of his eye.

Laurel touched his chin and drew his face toward hers. "I want a future with you, but I haven't been sure how you felt. I mean, after all that's happened. We haven't talked about it."

"I know. Too much has happened, too fast. There's so many things we have to consider." Jack cleared his throat and sat forward. "I have a surprise for you." He glanced back at Laurel, her eyes wide with anticipation. He chuckled and stood to retrieve an envelope from the mantel. "Your visa and your ITIN number came in the mail today."

"That's fantastic news." She reached out for the paper, unfolded it, and ran her fingers over the official seal.

"Now you have all the options. As soon as your passport gets here, you can go back to Scotland to find your mom. After that, you may decide to stay there. Or, maybe you'll decide to live in America. Maybe go to school here?" Jack shoved his hands in his pockets. "The difficulties start when you add me to the mix. My job is in Chicago, my family's in Montana. And then there's all the emotional stuff." Jack's gut twisted as he listed the complications.

Laurel pulled him back to the couch and leaned into him. Her lips hovered a breath away from his. "Let's just take it a day at a time."

Jack's senses charged to attention, and he slid his hand along Laurel's jaw. Cradling her face he drew her lips to his. She shifted, and he lifted her across his lap before pressing her back into the cushion and deepening the kiss. He ran his hand up her side and plunged his fingers into her hair.

"Or moment by moment." He murmured.

"I like that idea."

Jack searched her eyes and considered her. Laurel was strong, smart, and resourceful, but she was also innocent in many ways, especially with men. He wanted her, wanted to make love to her, but he didn't want to rush. Things were different in the real world. Most of all, Jack desired to protect her, to make sure she felt safe.

Laurel returned his gaze and a slow smile lit her

eyes. "What do you think about Tonya's offer for me to stay in the apartment above her salon? She thought I might like some—privacy."

"Smart woman."

A little giggle bubbled up her throat. "Maybe you'd like to have a spend-the-night sometime?"

A surge of pulsing heat enveloped him. His breath caught in his throat. Jack answered her with a kiss that communicated his desire. His hands worshiped her curves. Laurel drew him closer and pushed her body against his.

Electricity coursed through his system and it took all his self-discipline to pull back. He inhaled a deep breath. "Let's get you moved into Tonya's place first thing tomorrow."

CHAPTER 22

Moving didn't take long. All Laurel owned was one suitcase filled with hand-me-downs and a gaggle of department store bags.

"I'm glad to have someone using the space." Tonya poured Laurel a cup of coffee. "I'll have to get more tea. What kind do you like?"

Laurel smiled. It was so American to have a hundred types of tea. "Just black tea, for me, thanks."

"My schedule is filled up through the holidays, but it will be so nice to have someone to visit with between hair appointments." Tonya sat across from Laurel at the small kitchen dinette. "What's Jack up to today?"

"He's working with Trent at the ranch."

"I wish he'd move home. Half that ranch is his, you know." Tonya took a slow sip of her coffee. "It seems like he and Trent have worked through their issues, don't you think?"

"I don't know anything about it, really, but they seem like good chums."

Tonya nodded and a sweeping curl dropped over her eyes. She tossed her head. "There was some bad blood between them after their grandpa died. Jack left to go to West Point, then he joined the Army. He didn't come home again until this past fall. It's been over ten years."

Laurel wondered about Jack as a boy. She felt close to him, like she'd known him forever, but then there were times like this when she realized she hardly knew him at all. "I haven't been home in ten years either. I hope if we find my mam..." Laurel started again. "*When* we find her, that things go as smoothly between us as they seem to be going with Jack and his brothers. I still don't know if she wanted me to come back home or not."

"Of course she did." Tonya gave her an encouraging smile and rose to put her cup in the sink. The front bell jangled. "There's my ten o'clock. I'm staying in town for a Christmas Bazaar meeting tonight. Let's have dinner at Alice's. We can talk some more, and now that you have your visa, we can ask Alice if she has any work."

Flint River charmed Laurel when she stepped out of the salon after dark. White Christmas lights glowed in strings along Main Street and each old-fashioned street lamp was festooned with a wreath boasting a red bow. Snow drifted through the air and the effect was like a scene on a nostalgic a holiday card.

Laurel and Tonya walked, bundled in their warm coats, hats, and gloves, down to Alice's Diner. Even in the cold, people were out on the street. Everyone they passed greeted them and welcomed Laurel.

After their meal, Tonya asked Alice if she, by

chance, needed any holiday help.

"Sorry. I just hired a friend of Sadie's, a girl named Dakota."

"Shoot," Tonya murmured. "Have you heard if anyone else needs help?"

"In fact, Howard Stiltz over at the hotel said that they're running around like wild turkeys this year. He's hired one of his housekeeper's cousins to sing in the bar in the evenings. Says she's bringing in young people from all over who'd normally head into the city." Alice took up their empty plates. "Yep, I bet Howard could use an extra hand in the bar, or maybe with housekeeping. Let's ask him tonight at the planning meeting."

After Alice went back to the kitchen, Tonya put some bills on the table and stood. "What do you think about working at the hotel?"

"I'll take anything someone's willing to offer me, at this point."

Friday of that week, Laurel tied an apron around her uniform black skirt and white blouse. Her fingers flitted over the silver thistle charm that hung from her neck. She slipped an order pad in the apron pocket and made certain she had two pens. The time-clock stamped her card, and she was officially working at her new job.

Brad, the bartender, rushed into the kitchen with an order for a burger and fries. He turned to Laurel. "Don't worry, kiddo. You'll do fine. By the way, your first customer was just seated."

Laurel smiled at him, smoothed her skirt, and stepped through the swinging door into the bar. Jack sat at a table facing the stage. When he saw her, a grin lit his face.

"Hi." A strange shyness crept over Laurel and she felt herself blush, self-conscious of her lack of serving skills.

"Hey." Jack picked up the menu. "So what's good here?"

"I honestly don't know." Laurel bit her lower lip.

"Okay, how about I start with a beer? What's on tap?"

Jack stayed through the evening to listen to the new singer. Callie was from Tennessee and the notes dripped off her tongue like warm honey. Laurel enjoyed listening to her southern accent. Callie had wavy, dark-blonde hair that she dyed dark underneath. Five or six small, random braids were twisted throughout her hair, woven with different colors of string and beads.

A crowd gathered and stayed late to listen to the young woman sing and play her guitar. After Laurel's shift, she joined Jack for a final drink before closing time. They held hands while Callie strummed through her last set.

Jack scooted his chair close to Laurel's and draped his arm across the back. "You did great tonight. Think you're going to like the job?"

"It will serve its purpose." Laurel grinned. "But I don't think I'm meant to be a waitress for the long haul. I figure, since Tonya refuses to charge me rent, I'll have saved up for my plane ticket by the end of January."

"That gives me a little over a month to convince you to buy a round-trip ticket." The blue of Jack's eyes deepened and a thrill of energy bundled up in Laurel's body. She remembered Jack saying he would go to Scotland with her and she let her imagination wander to walking hand in hand with him through the Highlands.

"How's everything else going?" Jack leaned toward her and brought his hand up to the back of her neck. His thumb rubbed up and down. "Are you settled in at Tonya's? Do you need anything?"

His touch sent beads of heat into her core and she closed her eyes for several seconds, reveling in the sensations he stirred in her. "I'm fine, thanks. I've spent some time with Joscelyn."

"Good." Jack's gaze focused on her mouth. Distractedly, he asked, "You like her?"

"Aye, she's grand." Laurel laughed and Jack's eyes snapped up to hers. He smirked at getting caught staring at her lips. "Joscelyn's easy to talk to. She seems to understand my mixed-up feelings about my da." Laurel's mood dipped at the mention of her father.

Jack seemed to notice and took her hand.

"I showed her my sketchbook." Laurel peered intently at Jack wondering what he thought of that. He was the only other person who had ever seen her dark drawings.

Jack held her gaze and nodded slowly. "I think that's good. Joscelyn helped Cade deal with his horrific memories of being in the war. Maybe she can help you reconcile yours?"

"She said I could come to her anytime. That she would always be there for me, but she also gave me the number of a woman who is a therapist up in Missoula in case I wanted to talk to someone else, too."

"What did she say about the sketches?"

"She said it was a good thing I had a way to process things that happened to me and my feelings about them. I guess drawing is my way of dealing with the hard stuff." Laurel's cheeks pinked. "She saw my sketch of you, too."

"Yeah? What'd she say about that?"

"Not much. She just got a huge smile on her face and said, 'Oh, this is nice.' She mentioned that my last couple of drawings weren't as dark. She thinks that shows progress."

"Are you going to talk to her more about all that?"

"Aye, I think I will."

"Good. That's good." Jack reached up and brushed his fingers across Laurel's cheek. "I'm glad you connected with her."

"Me too. It's the first time I've been able to consider dealing with some of those memories."

Jack slid his arm over her shoulders and pulled her close. They sipped their drinks and settled back into the strums of Callie's guitar.

Laurel clenched her jaw and pressed into Jack's warmth for reassurance. "Jack, what if my mam doesn't want me to come home? Maybe she doesn't want me to find her."

Jack nodded. "Frankly, I'm not concerned about how she feels about it. You need to know, one way or the other, so you can move on with your life. We'll find her and hear her side of the story. It's the only way you'll truly be able to move forward."

Laurel shivered with misgiving against the unknown.

When the music ended, the lights brightened throughout the bar. Jack helped Laurel into her coat and walked her up Main Street to the front door of the salon. It was cold out, but neither seemed to notice as they spent the next half-hour kissing good-night in the lamplight.

Laurel didn't invite Jack in. Now that their lives were more settled and there weren't bullets flying at them or life-threatening storms raging over their heads, she wanted to slow down. Laurel knew she could trust Jack with her life. Now she wanted to learn if she could trust him with her heart.

CHAPTER 23

The week before Christmas had the Stone's house smelling like a bakery at the North Pole. Jack was sure he was breathing in sugar crystals and cinnamon with every breath. Laurel said she'd come out to the ranch in the morning to help Mary and the other women finish baking goodies for the Christmas Bazaar. He warmed at the thought of seeing her. Work was all he used to think about, his mind turning the details of open cases over constantly. Lately, his thoughts were consumed with Laurel and how they might navigate their future.

Bing Crosby crooned Christmas carols throughout the house as Jack and Trent hauled in a fresh-cut tree and set it up in the front window. Mary spread a hand-quilted tree skirt around the stand and stood back to admire the greenery. Jack inhaled the sharp pine scent laced with clove and ginger from the kitchen.

"We're here." Joscelyn called out as she entered the front door followed by Sadie, Cade, and Laurel.

Everyone carried boxes and bags. Jack rushed to take Laurel's load from her. He dumped everything in a chair and pulled her into his arms, kissing her.

"Morning." He said against her lips.

Laurel laughed. "Good morning." Her green eyes sparkled up at him.

"I missed you."

"Since last night?"

"Yes." He leaned into her ear. "You keep sending me home," he growled in a whisper.

"All right, you two. Break it up." Joscelyn took Laurel by the arm and led her into the kitchen. "We have work to do."

All day the house was merry with the family working and laughing together. Jack watched as all the people he cared about in the world shared laughter and love, drawing Laurel in as though she had always belonged. Late in the afternoon, Trent poured eggnog in small crystal tumblers and added whiskey to everyone's, but Sadie's. When he stopped pouring the amber liquid in Jack's, Jack nudged his glass forward for an extra splash.

He opened his arm to Laurel, and she nestled in. Jack took in the scene with his family gathered in the home where he grew up. It was a mess with baking dishes, cooling treats, wrapping paper and decorations scattered all over. He gazed down at the woman in his arm and knew, for the first time in his life, exactly what he wanted.

"Can I talk to you for a minute? Alone?" Jack said into Laurel's hair. She looked up at him with peace and joy in her eyes and nodded. He took her hand and led her out onto the front porch. She shivered and Jack pulled her into his arms.

"Everything all right?" she asked.

"Yes." He rested his chin on her head. "For the first time since I can remember, everything is exactly right." He pushed back so he could see her face. "Laurel." He tilted her chin up and gazed into her emerald eyes. "I'm in love with you."

Her eyes flared wide, and she smiled up at him. Jack bent down to kiss her. He drew back and searched her eyes. "I love you, Laurel MacNeil."

"I love you too, Jack Stone." Laurel stood on her toes and pressed her mouth to his. His heart burst with elation and his pulsed raced as he gathered her into his arms. Jack's head swam with joy and his body surged with desire. The freezing temperature outside couldn't touch them.

"Will you take me home?"

Heat flared throughout his body. "Yes. Laurel, I'll take you home tonight. I'll take you home to Scotland. And then, if you'll have me, I'll take you home forever."

ABOUT THE AUTHOR

Jodi Burnett is a Colorado native. She and her husband live on a small ranch southeast of Denver where she enjoys her horses, complains about her cows, and writes to create a home for her imaginings. In addition to loving life in the country, Jodi fosters her creative side by writing, painting with watercolor, quilting, and crafting stained-glass.

Join Jodi Burnett's Reader Group
And find out about new releases
at
Jodi-Burnett.com

Thank you for reading Danger In The Hills
by Jodi Burnett.

Please, kindly leave a review on
Amazon.com.

JODI BURNETT

DANGER IN THE HILLS

Made in the USA
Middletown, DE
10 September 2021